TODAY IS
ANOTHER
TOMORROW

TODAY IS ANOTHER TOMORROW

The Epic
Gone with the Wind
Parody

Missy D'Urberville

ST. MARTIN'S PRESS

NEW YORK

TODAY IS ANOTHER TOMORROW. Copyright © 1991 by Ben Metcalf and David Samuels.

Design by Glen M. Edelstein

Library of Congress Cataloging-in-Publication Data

D'Urberville, Missy.
    Today is another tomorrow : the epic Gone with the wind parody.
        p.   cm.
    ISBN 0-312-06565-5
    I. Title.
PS3554.U669T64   1991   813'.54—dc20   91-20918

First Edition: September 1991

10 9 8 7 6 5 4 3 2 1

There was a land of men who made a lot of money
working Ivy League graduates to death for what
my father pays his secretary per hour . . .

If these men were chivalrous,
I'm the Queen of Spain on a three-day vacation package
to Bally's Hotel and Casino in Las Vegas . . .

Here was the last ever to be seen
of those people
and their shirts with the little alligators on them . . .

Look for it only in books, for it
is no more than a dream remembered,
a civilization Gone with the Wind . . .

TODAY IS
ANOTHER
TOMORROW

Chapter
ONE

STARLIGHT O'Hara was not beautiful, but a girl can do a lot with herself these days if her father sits on the board of a firm as profitable as Wilkes Brothers O'Hara. Founded in 1881, the growth of Wilkes Brothers O'Hara was determined by one immutable and fundamental principle: As the number of Wilkeses and O'Haras increased, so did the number of Ivy League graduates the firm employed. Two of them sat by Starlight's side this sunny afternoon, admiring her Laura Ashley sundress and duckboots from L. L. Bean.

"Nice suit," one observed. "But what's with the Japanese man under the porch?"

"Oh," Starlight sighed. "That's Yamamoto. Daddy got him for us from some exchange program two years ago."

"Does he know English yet?" one or the other of them asked.

"No, but I think he wants to learn. The other day I

came home early and found him looking at the *Wall Street Journal*. Oooh," she exclaimed, playing with her long blonde hair, blonde because it's the best color for hair, "look at the beautiful sunset."

Towering above them stood Tarot, a house of astounding beauty. The sunlight illuminated the facade, its majestic yellow turning to radiant patches of blue and sudden starbursts of red in the world's only known example of tie-dyed Colonial architechture. This design, however, covered only half the house, its owner patiently awaiting the day when Ken Kesey and his Merry Pranksters would return to finish the job they had begun with such promise twenty years before.

Spring had come early this year to Scarsdale, with warm quick rains and a sudden frothing of empty McDonald's cartons and teenagers in knee-length shorts. It was an aggressively green land, from the Ortho-Gro green of the manicured front lawns, to the bright green of the Jaguars parked in front of the houses, to the sickly and pale green of the faces of the people who paid the bills.

"Look Starlight, about tomorrow," they said. "If you'll be our date to the Wilkes's barbecue, we'll tell you a secret."

"Oh!" Starlight said, rapt. "I love secrets, and even more knowing what they are."

"Well," said they, "you know Hashley Wilkes?"

"My boyfriend?" asked Starlight, dim memory creeping slowly to the front of her brain the way memories so often do.

"He's getting married on October fifteenth."

"To me?" asked Starlight.

"To Melody Hamilton."

2

What follows is the premiere episode of what I hope will satisfy the modern reader's insane craving for subplot, a foolish time- and space-wasting gimmick no author of romance can safely avoid these days.

Underneath the porch, Yamamoto pulled a cellular phone out of his jacket and dialed with a precision unheard of in the Western world.

"Hello?" answered a gruff voice.

"Yamamoto calling, my good man. Let us speak of chivalry."

"Do you know what time it is? It's four in the goddamn morning!"

"Chivalry, my learned friend. Is it true what they say, that it has died?"

"What the fuck kind of question is that?" growled the voice on the other end. He did not wait for an answer.

A long time ago, before the book began, Jerry O'Hara had ridden over to the Wilkes compound to borrow some food. Jerry would claim to have no recollection of his movements, and Starlight would know in her heart of hearts he was telling the truth. She would browbeat him nonetheless and hope the others would not catch on, would never discover that her father did not remember yesterday, any of them.

The dark cedars that lined the smoothly paved driveway to Tarot had been relocated from elsewhere on the grounds to clear land for Jerry's gardening, the only activity he gave himself over to completely. While their gnarled arms met in a crude arch overhead, turning the long and winding avenue into a dim and frightening tunnel, the cedars provided a natural barrier between Tarot's gardens and the police and Jerry could not be convinced to tear them down.

Starlight hurried through the passageway and knelt behind a clump of bushes to change her clothes and await her father's return. *He'll tell me I've dreamed the whole thing up,* she thought, *that there's no truth to any of it, that the Wilkeses are merely a joke between him and my mother.*

Growing up, Hashley Wilkes had seemed so very uninteresting. But what had been boring then had matured into savoir faire, a knowing acceptance of everything around him. Nothing shocked him, nothing surprised him, very little passed through his field of vision that provoked even the slightest flickering of his eyes—mild, peaceful, and tightly closed.

Oh, why was he so blasé about their relationship, so distant? Why do men ignore the women who love them, men with such blond-colored hair? The very blondness of him excited her curiosity like a door that had neither knobs nor hinges, a doorway with no door. And now, like some terrible flatulence, had come the news. Hashley to marry Melody!

He came over the rise at breakneck speed, leaning back so far on his long, low chopper that from a distance he appeared to be sleeping. She would have to act quickly, would have to leave the world of thought behind.

"Stop you fool! Stop! You live here!" she screamed, leaping up from behind the bushes and running out into the road. In an attempt to avoid hitting what he mistook for a raccoon and her children, Jerry fell off his mount and skidded nearly thirty yards in a sitting position before gaining his feet. The bike jumped the ditch, wrapped itself around a cedar, and exploded. By the time Starlight

4

reached her father he was operating on primordial instinct alone.

"Get the fuck off my property, man," Jerry screamed, "I know my rights, and I don't have to take shit like this from anybody, man. Unless I see a warrant first . . ."

"Oh, don't be silly! Of course I don't have a warrant!" Starlight responded, hurt.

"Then I'll have to ask you to leave, man—this is private property."

"I know. I live here. It's me . . . Starlight."

Jerry O'Hara was sixty years old with a hatfull of crisp curly silver-white hair that once, long ago, had been blond. His perpetually confused face was deeply grooved and ancient, fearfully dark hollow pits having long ago replaced the beady blue eyes once young with the unworried youthfulness of one who has never taxed his brain with dangerous chemicals. And yet, beneath his choleric exterior glowed the faintest coal of recognition.

"Your daughter," she reiterated, "your eldest daughter."

"Oh, yeah . . ." he said, embracing her tightly. "Hey man, welcome home—how're things over at the Wilkes's?"

She slipped her arm through his and began leading him up the winding driveway to Tarot. She knew that any attempt to retrieve information from her father was utterly useless and yet, looking at him in the fading light, she found it comforting to be in his presence. There was something vital, earthy, and coarse about him that she found distasteful, but he was easily the richest man in town.

"There it is, man," said Jerry, as Starlight's guests waved good-bye from their twin red Porsche 911s. "The fun is over, the crowd goes home."

"What are you babbling about?" Starlight asked gently.

"The kids, man," Jerry responded, suddenly passionate. "They gave up. Went home."

"On what?"

"Buses, trains . . ."

"No, Daddy. Gave up on what?"

"The revolution, man. They let us down."

"Jesus, Daddy," sighed Starlight as what little light remained struggled to shine through the cedar canopy above their heads. "I'm sick and tired of you talking about how great the sixties were. Why, just name one thing kids had in the sixties that they don't have now."

"Tear gas," Jerry responded, choked with emotion. "It just ain't the same party without tear gas, man."

They proceeded inside and spent the next eight and a half hours watching television.

Chapter
TWO

LIKE dubious Paris fallen in battle, Starlight's black party dress, a Givenchy original, lay sprawled across the bed, badly in need of a good cleaning. The form upon which it was stretched lay equally motionless, but not for long.

"Bacon and eggs, jus' how you likes it!" Chamois announced, busting through the door. The reader no doubt recognizes how difficult it is to find, much less keep, good help these days. Chamois was the best the Wilkeses could do in today's troubled labor market. Her speech, normal in other respects, appeared phonetically on the printed page, as if by magic.

"My, my, my," she said, "you look so pretty today, jus' like one ob dem Franz Kline pictures ol' Chamois have up in her room."

"Chamois," Starlight whined, "you know I hate bacon and eggs. Take them back."

"Ol' Chamois slabe and slabe for the white chillums

all her life, she should know by now to expect dis kine ob selfish ingratitude. But as long as I libs, I guess I still ain't used to it.''

"I hate being such a fat pig!"

"I hates lots o things, honey," Chamois said, hands on her hips, "but one tries as one do to make de very best of what one hates, even when it ain't pretty and won't eats its breakfas'." Stretching out on Starlight's bed, Chamois began to attack the meal with a vengeance.

"Could you at least get me some Corn Flakes?" Starlight pleaded, "Corn Flakes with milk?"

"Black folk hab no truck wid Corn Flakes," Chamois declared. "Dat's slabe food, and ol' Chamois ain't goin' to fetch no slabe food for some girl what make her ol' mammy eat her breakfas' for her."

"Slave food?"

"Back in de South, massa makes the slabes eat Corn Flakes and milk for ebry meal 'til they was done sick ob dere libes and plead wid almightly God fo' deliberance. Yessir. And before they sells a slabe, massa gibs them slice o' toas', orange juice, and coffee too. That's why you won't catch ol' Chamois bringin' none o' that to yo' door, neither," she continued as Starlight stomped angrily from the room. "What dey teach kids in school nowadays sho' is a mystery to me."

Chamois stretched out on the bed and thought of the day that lay ahead. The Wilkes Brothers barbecue was the one family event of the year for the O'Haras, and every year it was different. Some years, Jerry would refuse to leave the house. Others, he would refuse to come home, addressing the Wilkeses by the names of his daughters and falling asleep on their bathroom floor. Last year he made it all the way to the driveway, where he

8

sat until Chamois called the police to report a prowler.

It was no wonder that the girls had turned out the way they had, Chamois reflected. Starlight was like Hancock tower—steel and glass with large pieces missing upstairs. Sioux-Ellen walked around the house muttering the words to "The Circle Game."

It hadn't always been this way. When Chamois first arrived, Starlight had been a gurgling four-year-old who tampered with the caps on childproof bottles. And now . . .

Children are such a pain in the ass.

The door swung open, and Starlight entered the room as Chamois quickly finished up the last bits of bacon left on the breakfast tray in front of her. "Whas' goin' on, chile?" Chamois asked, beaming. "You all ready fo' yo' big day?"

"Chamois!" Starlight exclaimed, stamping her foot with the impetuousness of youth. "Stop teasing me or I'll have you deported."

"Only person deported is de man yo school name after, deported by de English fo' crimes make you sick to eben' think on. No, ol' Chamois jus' another ignorant black folk, like Martin Luther King or one a those LL Cool-Man peoples you listens to on the stereo."

Starlight sat down on the bed, head downcast. "Oh Chamois," she sighed, "why are men so insensitive?"

"Mens and womens jus' sees different, I expects. Woman look at a man, she see long nights, she see li'l babies, she see a big ol' house wid' all de kitchen appliances. Man look at a woman and he see another woman standin' behind her wid' a tight butt. Dat's de game, long as Chamois watch it played."

"That's the old days, Chamois," Starlight objected. "Men today are sensitive."

"Sho' dey sensitive. Men always sensitive. And it be in one place honey, and dat place be the same since time began."

"But surely there are men who don't think that way anymore."

"Yes, chile, dey are. Dey on TV, dat's all."

"I don't care!" Starlight wailed. "I love Hashley. I'll die if Melody Hamilton gets him. Please," Starlight pleaded, "tell me what men like."

"Dat be different fo' eb'ry man," Chamois decisively replied. "Some likes one thing, some likes another."

"What do you think Hashley likes?"

Chamois looked Starlight up and down. "You know how to leave town tomorrow? I expects dat sabe eb'ry-one trouble all around."

Shortly after breakfast, Jerry was found wandering in his gardens. He had cut his left foot badly and there was no way of knowing how much blood he had lost. Under normal circumstances, he would have been ignored until it was time for the barbeque, but Starlight had it on good authority that Yamamoto was "bowshit 'bout sumpfin'—fixin' to resine," and she thought her father should at least be present when he did.

Yamamoto came down the staircase wearing his cashmere overcoat and silk bowler, a suitcase in each calfskin-leathered hand. He walked over to where Starlight, Jerry, Sioux-Ellen, and Chamois were waiting, scanned their startled faces, and began to speak.

"Living and working in this household has been the most humiliating experience of my entire life. My time here was monopolized to the extent that I was forced to dishonor my family name by taking two years to do what any other competent Japanese man could have done in one."

"Wha's dat?" Chamois asked.

"Get a doctorate in business administration from Columbia University," he replied, walking past them toward the door.

The sight of the one other male at Tarot touched a nerve deep in Jerry's psyche, prompting him to speak. His curiosity knew no bounds. "Hey, man, what's in the bags?"

"These suitcases contain my doctoral thesis notes," Yamamoto replied. "My thesis, you may find it interesting to know, is largely concerned with rampant illicit collusion in today's investment banking industry. All three of the professors who reviewed it have been sitting on your board of directors for years. None of them seemed at all surprised by my results, and they were quite eager to see that I received the highest marks possible."

"Open the bag, man," said Jerry, walking toward Yamamoto with outstretched arms. "Share and share alike."

"Wrong," Yamamoto replied, putting down his luggage and straight-arming Jerry. "Let me also say that I did not eat your drugs; I merely pretended so I could inconspicuously spend most of the day under the front porch, working on my dissertation. To say that I've had enough of this family after two years would be to mislead you. I was sick of you the day I moved in."

The O'Hara's watched in stunned silence as Yamamoto picked up his bags and left Tarot. Chamois alone took Yamamoto's departure well, remaining calm except for a single outburst of wild applause at the end of his speech.

**The O'Haras watched in stunned silence as
Yamamoto picked up his bags and left Tarot.**

"I can't fuckin' believe this, man," Jerry said with a tear in his eyes. "Those guys really do learn faster."

In the East, it is said that a pound of cure often works.

Hurt that his daughters did not want to ride on his new motorcycle, Jerry could not be talked out of driving to the Wilkes's in his VW bus. Like those of us who have known the pleasures of automobile ownership, he felt his vehicle to be superior to all others. Sioux-Ellen was certain her father was going to get them all killed.

"Slow the fuck down, Dad!" she screamed as he took a curve at breakneck speed.

"Hey, man," he assured her, "two wheels on the ground is all it takes."

Starlight sat in the back of the bus, unaware of the fuss in front, lost in deepest contemplation. The thoughts galloping through her brain were deep and many-faceted, unintelligible to all but the most skilled lip-reader:

I wonder, she thought, *what Daddy will think when I tell him Hashley and I are to be married. I don't think there'll be much of a personality problem—Hashley has always thought Daddy was sort of fun to have around and Daddy will just forget who Hashley is, as he always does. They're actually a lot alike, if you think about it. They both went to Yale, although I don't think Daddy remembers that he went to college at all. But Hashley might be able to describe it to him, and that would at least keep him talking for a while. They both have blond hair and blue eyes, at least Daddy's used to be blond before that Owsley person made the basement explode. And even though Hashley doesn't have a drug problem like Daddy, his eyes do roll back in his head when you talk to him—*

A loud *thump* and a blood-curdling scream from her sister directed Starlight's attention to the front of the bus.

13

"The Wilkes's dog! You just ran over the Wilkes's dog!"

"It was a turtle, man—I heard the shell crack."

"Really, Sioux," Starlight interjected. "It's not like the Wilkeses can't afford another one, and Daddy's doing the best he can; leave him alone before your screaming gets us all killed."

Playing the martyr as sisters do, Sioux-Ellen turned back around in her seat and sulked while Jerry treated them to a slightly off-key and largely unintelligible rendition of "White Rabbit." As they reached the private drive to the Wilkes compound, however, he stopped singing.

"Girls," he said, slowing down slightly to make the turn into the driveway, "you know how much this party means to the Wilkeses, right? Well, I'd really hate to spoil it, man. I say we wait till it's over to tell them about their turtle, OK?"

Why can't family members be honest with each other?

Lying on his waterbed high atop the Scarsdale Hilton, Yamamoto produced his cellular phone and dialed the same number he had dialed the day before.

"What?" growled the voice. "Who is it?"

"Just me, my good man. Let us speak of self-delusion and the end of empire on this fine afternoon."

"Why bother?"

"I feel I've had a breakthrough. Been fooling myself for so long, you know, but all that's changed now."

"What's changed?"

"Good God, Man!" screamed Yamamoto. "You've got a point. How soon can you get over here?"

The man on the other end laughed, but said nothing.

14

Chapter
THREE

A good friend of mine, who was into Zen before it was cool, is fond of saying "The things we have are often the things we value least." As the VW microbus pulled into the circular drive just inside the compound's walls, Starlight valued the parked cars and felt a rush of hot shame. When they came to a sudden, crashing halt behind them, however, the advantage of her father's steadfast insistence on taking the VW became clear. While each of the other vehicles had sustained thousands of dollars in damage, the aging microbus looked much the same as it had the day before.

"Yer gonna just die when you see this party—Dadda's completely outdone himself," shrieked India Wilkes, Hashley's little sister. "He even got a Kennedy!"

"A what?" asked Starlight, pushing her way through the cocktail-sipping crowd in the front hall and into the immense ballroom, where several hundred glamorous

Ivy League graduates nibbled on hors d'oeuvres, sipped champagne, and chatted on cellular phones. Towering above the guests for the usual symbolic reasons stood a huge golden calf. Its perked ears brushed the thirty-foot-high ceiling. Its stout legs spread across nearly half the straw-covered floor.

"Starlight!" yelled a pale young investment banker who had but little time left to live. "Charles! Charles Hamilton! Do you get into the city much? Got to hook up for lunch one day—"

A tap on the shoulder provided Starlight with an opportunity to banish the Hamilton boy, bringing her face-to-face with Emmy Slandery, the *New York Post*'s society reporter and Starlight's archenemy at Phillips Exeter Academy.

"Good evening, Miss O'Hara," Slandery began, holding out a small tape recorder. "Are you aware that Japanese investors disclosed this morning that they have accumulated approximately ten percent of the openly traded stock in several major U.S.—"

A loud crash from somewhere behind the house cut her short. By the time Starlight and the others had reached the backyard, both driver and passenger were out of the pool. The driver, seeing no means of escape at his disposal, lumbered toward the startled guests.

"I dove, musta dove three or four times," he babbled, "I couldn't get the back door open, that's all. It's not my fault she left her pocketbook down there. I did what I could."

"That's him," whispered Emmy, close on Starlight's heels, "That's Bubba Kennedy!"

"There's one piece of America those Japs'll never

Towering above the guests for the usual symbolic
reasons stood a huge golden calf.

17

own!" yelled Sioux-Ellen, prompting a moment of dead silence from the crowd.

"Damn straight!" Starlight yelled. "We beat the pants off that Hitler before, and we can damn well do it again."

"Hitler is dead, man," called Jerry from the shallow end, where he was wading naked from the waist down. "And we're all responsible."

"Well, you know, a lot has changed since then," chirped India.

"More than you think, girls!" shouted a grating, high-pitched male voice through the din. "My name," the man continued, stroking an absurdly thin mustache, "is Brett Butler." He was easily the best man at the party, with an air that suggested he was waiting for an important phone call.

"There is something I really must know," Butler continued. "Has even one of you considered the fact that there's not a single Fortune Five Hundred company without at least one Japanese citizen on its board of directors? If just one of you will step forward and admit that you haven't laid eyes on a functioning factory in the United States, I will be able to comfort myself with the thought that you are not all idiots."

"It's true," came a meek shout from somewhere to Starlight's right. It was her brave Hashley, with that Melody Hamilton by his side in a Benetton rip-off. "I've never seen a factory in my life."

Butler stared contemptuously at Hashley for a moment then once again addressed the crowd: "If just one more of you will step forward, I will rest assured that not all of you are fools." When there came no response from the crowd, he snorted at them and said, "In that case, ladies and gentlemen, you'll excuse me."

18

Clicking his heels and murmuring obscenities he vanished into thin air as a hundred half-serious threats of physical violence filled the yard. In the confusion that followed, Starlight slipped into the house, slammed her head against the doorpost, and knocked herself unconscious.

Blurry form: two waving arms, two heads, one long leg: Love. Why she loved the two-headed blurry creature with one leg she could not say. All she knew was that she had to make her feelings known, it must take her in its arms and never let her go.

At the touch of its hand, she began to tremble. It was going to happen now, just as she had dreamed it. The form blurred again and resolved itself, the twin heads being replaced by a single one with less hair and fewer limbs but no less beautiful for that. Hashley!

"I called a cab," he said nervously, thrusting a piece of paper toward her. "Keep the change."

Unsteadily she rose to her feet, a light gleaming in her eye. "I . . . I love you, Hashley."

For an instant there was a silence so acute that neither dared speak, a stiff ceremonial silence like one that follows the videotaped explosion of a 747 on the six o'clock news. Then the trembling, the fear fell away. Why hadn't she just said these few words before? How simple it was. Her eyes sought his, her hands fumbled at the buttons on her dress.

Hashley gazed deeply back, backing away, his mouth moving but no sound coming out. There was a look of consternation in his eyes, of incredulity, of something more. And why was Hashley making those odd gurgling noises like a baby having trouble with its food? Then something like a well-trained mask or paper bag descended over his face, he stood up, and smiled gallantly.

19

"Wonderful day we're having, Starlight. Wonderful day. Good weather. Very good day for this kind of weather, what?" He bowed and extended his hand, an invitation to dance.

"Hashley?"

"It is wonderful, isn't it. I love the wisteria when it's in bloom. It was mother's favorite, when she was alive."

Something was wrong, all wrong! But what?

"Hashley," Starlight responded softly, "your mother is outside, with the children near the golden calf."

"Ah, mother. She loved ponds so. She loved the changing of the leaves, the sweet music of the frogs and the crickets at night, the crackle of a roaring fire on a cold evening." His mouth was working furiously, the whites of his eyes upturned.

"Yes, dear," Starlight answered. "You know I love you."

At this Hashley shuddered a bit before once again the mask fell with a thud over his pale white features. "My mother," he said with an air of calm exposition, "my mother was a saint. St. Thomas Aquinas, to be exact. If you look carefully, the resemblance about the nose and mouth is really quite striking," he continued. "She loved a fire on a cold winter's day."

"Hashley!" Starlight gasped, overjoyed to see some sign of passion beneath his cool, well-groomed exterior. "Hashley, I love you. I want us to live together until we die!"

"Starlight, you must never speak of these things with me again." His face was grim, fierce. "You'll hate me for hearing them."

"You do love me!" she exclaimed. Hashley was beginning to lose patience.

"No. No, I don't."

"Are you sure?"

Hashley thought for a moment. "Well, what do you mean by 'love'?"

"Do you miss me when I'm not around?"

Hashley thought for a moment. "No."

"Do you ever have moments when you couldn't bear to be alive?"

"Now."

Starlight pursed her lips. "Why don't you say it, coward," she exclaimed, the blind anger of her Irish forebears coming through, the same blind anger that led them to declare war on the British when the British were better equipped, stronger, and more numerous than they. "You want . . . you want . . ." What was the word she was looking for? Oh yes. "Happiness. How dare you?"

"Starlight, please . . ."

He put out his hand and as he did she reached back and slapped him across the face with all the power ten years of backhands at the club had given her. He said nothing, wiping the blood from his mouth. Then he was gone, before she could slap him again—a trail of blood on the Bloomingdale's carpet beside her the only reminder that he had, for however long, remembered her name. Now he would remember her name forever, the crazy girl, the one that hit me in the face.

I'm as bad as Honey Wilkes, she thought suddenly, remembering the poor girl who lived in the attic and told male visitors she loved them until someone brought her back upstairs and locked her inside.

Brett Butler materialized in the lobby of the Scarsdale Hilton and took the elevator up to the penthouse suite.

"My friend!" exclaimed Yamamoto, letting him in. "And what shall we speak of today?"

21

"Money," said Butler flatly, handing his host an invoice for services rendered.

"They say that money cannot buy you love," said Yamamoto, producing his checkbook.

"When you have enough money," said Butler, stroking his mustache and checking the figure over Yamamoto's shoulder, "the love comes free, like Pan Am bonus miles."

The sound of clicking heels abruptly snapped Starlight from her reverie. When she looked up, Brett stood before her.

He paused for a moment and studied Starlight through the black-rimmed monocle that hung from the lapel of his black textured Armani suit. "Ah, what have we here?" he asked, his heavy hands hanging limply by his side. "A little firebrand, a firecracker."

Her temper was beginning to rise at the thought of being humiliated by yet another man, this time one she didn't like, not even a bit. The thought that he had witnessed her run-in with Hashley was more than she could bear. So often is the shame we can least bear the shame most seen!

"You, sir, are no gentleman!" Starlight indignantly sputtered.

"True enough," he allowed. "I am vice president in charge of the foreign exchange desk at Wilkes Brothers, O'Hara, with a salary larger than the combined income of the Jacksons for the Victory tour. I own property in seven countries—eight if you count Canada. I'm worth more than the Victoria diamond and while that doesn't mean I'm a gentleman, it ensures I can go wherever a gentleman goes and get far better service."

22

"Oooh," Starlight softly allowed.

"And let me also say that you, miss, are no lady. But you are a girl of rare tenacity, however misguided. I take off my hat to you."

If she could have killed him she would have done so, but she knew Wilkes Brothers would be nowhere without him, her inheritance ruined. Wordlessly, she walked out of the room and slammed the door behind her.

She ascended the stairs with such swiftness that almost no time had passed before she reached the landing. Through the wide bay window on the lawn she could see the men still lounging in their chairs, scratching their heads, marveling at the window placed there instead of in a more conventional setting. How she envied them!

She heard the low hum of a BMW in the front drive, the slamming of a cellular phone in its cradle, and the sound of excited voices below. A man got out of the car and the crowd swarmed about him, plastic champagne glasses and the wicker baskets from the buffet abandoned on the lawn. In spite of the distance she could hear the cacophony of voices, questioning, wondering, calling their brokers. Then above the chaos came the voice of John Wilkes, clear and strong.

"Takeover!" he shouted, "The Japs have filed with the SEC!" As she watched, the guests jumped into their cars and peeled out of the driveway to do battle with the foreign invader.

In the midst of the sudden chaos that descended over the party, Starlight had but a single concern: to find an empty room and lock herself inside. Her heart was quiet now, and she figured she could slip into the deserted ballroom without being detected. Carefully, she eased open the door of the dressing room, only to run smack into Charles Hamilton.

"There's a trade war on now," he whispered.

"Oh," Starlight answered, uninterested.

"But that's not really what's on my mind."

"What is?" Starlight asked, glancing nervously toward the dressing room door. Did Charles too know of her shame?

"It's a merger I'm thinking about," he continued, his face drawing closer to hers, "a merger that would leave a surplus on the benefit side that would make the Texaco takeover look sick. The market being what it is," he added plaintively, "dare I hope the balance sheet might be in my favor?"

"Charles, whatever are you talking about?"

"Futures—our future, to be precise," he answered, "ensured by the only tie that lasts: a prenuptial agreement signed by both parties and recognized as binding by a court of law."

Starlight looked away for a moment and sighed.

"Of course I'll be away on business for the firm for a few months and will only be home on weekends, but a horizontally integrated union like ours should be able to survive whatever the market might throw our way."

Starlight sighed again. "Fine," she answered, still unsure of what he was trying to say, but hoping to hear no more of it.

"My darling!" Charles yelled, overjoyed. "I'll have my secretary fax you the papers first thing in the morning before I fly to Tokyo."

Outside, the roses bloomed and the sun shone brilliantly through the clouds. Birds chirped and dogs barked at their owners. Oh, to be young and in love!

Chapter
FOUR

IT'S impossible to get the tops off these childproof jars. This fact was perhaps the furthest thing from Starlight's mind in the last days of April 1985. Starlight was busy, busier than I've been in weeks. Events were jumbled together with a combination of craft and logic unseen since my last Lean Cuisine dinner. Especially vague were Starlight's recollections of the time between her acceptance of Charles and their double wedding with Hashley and Melody.

Time being of the essence, the whole of Starlight's not inconsiderable network of sorority sisters, prep school boyfriends, and half-remembered playgroup companions was called upon to ensure a successful outcome to the nuptials: a top-of-the-fold announcement in *The New York Times*.

Before she knew it, Starlight was clad in her mother's wedding dress (early-period Halston) and veil (by Matsuda), ready to descend the main staircase at Tarot on her father's arm to face a house filled with guests and tables of Sterno-warmed hors d'oeuvres. If only life went so smoothly for the rest of us!

It was all very dreamlike, the passage through the aisle of smiling faces, Charles's scarlet cheeks and stammering replies, the way Starlight's eyes stayed tightly shut throughout the affair. And like a half-remembered dream there were inexplicable things that nonetheless were there, like Charles.

"What's your issue?" a reporter yelled at Starlight, startling her from her reverie.

"Isn't it a bit early for that?" Starlight asked.

The reporter sighed. "The issue you're concerned about. The reason you're having this party."

Starlight's answer was drowned out by a roar from the platform where the wedding couples were to exchange vows. "Alright, let's have some quiet here!" a short, balding man with a Vandyke beard bellowed into a bullhorn. "Mrs. Feldman, please. I'm not your father. This is neither the time nor the place to work out your hostilities toward authority. Mr. Ross, talking to your neighbor is no substitute for adequate sexual performance; I'd think you'd have learned that by now." Conversation abruptly ceased.

"Thank you." He cleared his throat. "I'm known to many of you in a professional capacity as Dr. Mead. As I look around this beautiful garden on this happy occasion and see all of your smiling faces, full of hope and good wishes for the soon-to-be-betrothed, I can only be reminded of the strange paths upon which life may take us, the broken homes, the unresolved oedipal complexes, the many forms of unnatural, deviant behavior, which I will reveal to everyone present if you are not all quiet during the ceremony. And yes, I think of the soon-to-be-betrothed themselves, so radiant in their wedding clothes.

26

They have always been there for me, just as Starlight's pathological exhibitionism and Hashley's inability to cope with pressures that most people would consider normal parts of everyday life will be there for them in the years to come."

Dr. Mead turned toward the two wedding couples. "Hashley and Charles, take the hands of your betrothed." The grooms responded with alacrity. "You are frail creatures as are we all, the miserable droppings of constipated Nature. You hold the hands of your beloved within your own, a thin envelope of blood, calcium, and grease providing an infinitesimal amount of heat energy, a mild quickening of sluggish blood, the unsteady palpitation of a weakened heart. Already, the process of decay has set in. You may now kiss the brides."

A short month later, Starlight remembered little of Doc Mead's speech or what had transpired afterward. All she had to remind her of her wedding day was a book of press clippings and a single sheet of heat-sensitive fax paper:

WILKESBROS.TOKYO14:29

Sorry to advise husband Charles no longer on payroll. Will return body by Federal Express; pager and laptop remain property of the firm. May it console you that Mr. Hamilton made great sacrifice for reasons that will become clear in subsequent chapters. I am, Madam, the vice president in charge of foreign operations.

Brett Butler
Wilkes Bros./O'Hara

P.S. You love me.

At least in a novel, if the guy gets in the way of the plot, the author can off him. In life, there are laws.

Chamois was kind and comforting when made privy to the potentially devastating information, but she immediately packed her bags and left on an extended vacation when it became apparent that Starlight had no intention of leaving Tarot after the child was born. When the time came, Starlight quietly checked into neighboring Port Charles's General Hospital under an assumed name, paid cash in advance, and experienced a smooth delivery thanks to the wonders of modern medical technology.

When Starlight explained to her father that she and her child were leaving Tarot to stay with her Aunt Pat Hamilton, the only member of her late husband's family who would return her calls, he let her know he had serious reservations.

"It's not that I don't like the dude," Jerry said, lifting his torn Leon Trotsky T-shirt to scratch his round, hairy belly. "I just think he's a little young for you, man. You should shop around."

As she sat on the train to the City, the Sharper Image bassinet beside her, she considered Jerry's words. Perhaps she did need to be a bit more discriminate when it came to the men in her life. In a fit of acute panic, she resolved to ask the man sitting across from her for advice.

"Excuse me, sir," she said, gaining his attention and causing him to lower the paper he was reading, "may I ask to what profession you belong?"

"I'm a film producer," he said, raising his paper and hoping to be left alone.

"Do you live in the City?" The man peered at her peculiarly above his paper, one eyebrow raised.

"Doesn't everyone?"

"Well, you see I'm moving there now and I was wondering if you might have some advice for me concerning my demeanor. My name is Starlight O'Hara and I . . ."

The man dropped his paper completely, a gleeful look in his eyes.

"What did you say your name was, young lady?"

"Starlight. Starlight O'Hara."

"My advice then," he said, laughing quite hard, "is to dump the kid, just cut him right out."

"Sir, I fail to see the humor in . . ."

"Trust me, trust me," the man squealed, holding his sides. "You will marry a tall, dark stranger with the most passé mustache and . . . Oh, if you'll excuse me. Best of luck, my dear."

The man got up and walked to the front of the car, where he sat down and resumed reading his paper, chuckling to himself all the while. When the train pulled into Grand Central she departed quickly, hoping to get as far away from the disturbing stranger as possible.

Arriving by cab at Aunt Pat's building on Madison and Seventy-third, Starlight was exhausted and near tears. Yet, stepping into the lobby, she realized that the New York she had longed to see was small indeed compared to the real thing. The immense Jochen Gerz sculpture that served as the lobby's centerpiece was the most downright tasteful thing she had ever seen in her life, and the track lighting poised above it caught positively every nuance of the rough, inscribed surface. But even as she marveled at the decor, she had the distinct feeling that this picture was not complete, that something was missing, something important.

The baby! There was no time now—the child was lost forever and she would simply have to accept the guilt of having failed as a mother.

"And what shall entertain our thoughts today?" asked Yamamoto as he floated on a raft in the Hilton pool, sipping mint julep.

"Marriage," yelled Butler, executing a flawless triple gainer with a twist.

"Perhaps it is a bit early for us to discuss marriage," chuckled Yamamoto when his friend resurfaced.

"Marriage," said Butler, getting out of the water and drying himself with an unintentional click of his heels, "is like a head-on collision—it's hard to say who's to blame, and harder still to get out alive."

"How did you do that?"

"It's simple. Here, I'll do another one: Marriage is like a bad meal—"

"No, no—how did you become dry?"

Chapter
FIVE

DESPITE the violent crimes so often reported in the media, New York remains a wonderful city to visit, for a lazy afternoon or an evening out on the town. Literally hundreds of galleries, thousands of restaurants, and millions of people await the visitor. "Hundreds of galleries, thousands of restaurants, millions of people," Starlight enthused. "You could live here forever and do something new and different every night."

"It is a problem," Pat concurred.

"Problem?" Starlight asked. "I find it rather exciting."

"Danger is always exciting from afar," Pat explained. "Up close it's a different story."

"Aunt Pat?" Starlight asked. "What could possibly be wrong with taking advantage of all the city has to offer?"

"Everyone does it," Pat explained, fixing Starlight with a steely gaze.

"I see," Starlight replied. "But what about the little

things, like ordering Chinese food at midnight and eating it from the carton?"

"What I said goes for all the simple pleasures."

"Like sex?" Starlight asked.

"If millions of small-town teenagers do it," Pat said, "you don't."

"What can I do?"

"Take dance classes, get your hair done, and go out for dinner."

Starlight breathed a sigh of relief. A new world was opening its arms to her, and while it was a much less interesting world than she had imagined it to be an hour ago, at least she'd never have to ask for directions.

Pat returned from the kitchen, all smiles. "Everything is set," she declared. "We have appointments with Kenneth, tickets for the AIDS benefit—"

"It's wonderful that you're so deeply concerned about society," Starlight said.

"Everyone in society is concerned," Pat replied. "If this disease gets any worse, there won't be a thing to wear."

Starlight stared admiringly at her aunt. She seemed to have it all: the right friends, the right addresses, all the right stuff. Pat was a woman with total access, but something was missing, a name, a place, an intangible something . . .

"A job," Starlight blurted. "You don't have a job."

"Millions of people don't have jobs," Pat replied. "If you're not careful, they ask you for money on the street."

"But don't you feel like you should be doing something?"

"Now? I never lunch before one," Pat said.

"But what about a career?" Starlight asked. "Don't you need a career to be a liberated woman?"

"I'm completely liberated," Pat answered. "My children live in LA, my husband is dead, Susie does the housework, and my accountant pays the bills. And if that doesn't make me liberated, I don't know what would."

In the Montparnasse section of Paris, Yamamoto sat in a clean, well-lighted place and sipped his julep.

"The rich are different than you and me," he said.

"Yes," his friend Butler replied, "they owe more money."

The foci of the restaurant/space were three rather small tables, each adorned with but a single rose. Above the stage, huge cranes moved the last four Oscar-winning directors wherever they wanted to go. Starlight found Pat sitting near the edge of the stage, dress pulled up to afford David Lynch a better view of the mule tattoed on her upper thigh.

"Pat," she said, seating herself, "What's going on here? Is there a movie being made?"

"Don't be naive. There are several being made."

"You mean—"

"Exactly. You can't name one important recent film that doesn't have at least one scene in a classy New York eatery. This place can look like any of them, if shot from the right angle."

"What do the actors get out of it?"

"They eat for free and get paid for each appearance. Dustin and Diane get a cool million every time they walk in the door. There's always a need for shots of them in Manhattan restaurants."

"Then how do they make money?"

"By letting us in, silly. Hope you brought your Platinum Card."

"Never mind that," came a voice from above, "I brought mine."

Oliver Stone's crane momentarily lowered onto the stage and off stepped Brett Butler, waving farewell to his ride.

"I do hope you ladies will allow me to join you," he began, taking a seat. "I'm afraid I've got serious matters on my mind, though. Waiter!"

"Yes, sir."

"How much is the twenty-three Mouton-Cadet."

"One hundred and fifty."

"A bottle?"

"A glass. We rarely have requests for it by the bottle, sir."

"We'll take three." Brett turned back to his companions and sighed. "The economy is buckling at the seams. Foreign money is pouring into this country like a quart of bourbon down John Tower's throat. And if there's one thing you can believe about these foreigners it's that their accountants are better than ours."

"Ahem," managed the waiter, "may I help you?"

"An appetizer of some kind, with gold sauce," Brett said. The waiter stood there, stunned. "What's the matter, you deaf?"

"I'm your waiter, you *moron*! Whadayawanori'lltrowyouse *out*!"

The surrounding tables erupted in wild applause. John Hughes's crane lowered him, teary-eyed, onto the stage, where he embraced the waiter and lauded his brilliant, comi-tragic portrayal of a young man trapped between duty and humiliation. Only then did the trio realize their waiter was the great Robert DeNiro.

"Keep those cameras rolling, dammit," screamed Brett, leaping up and quickly bringing DeNiro to his knees with a pressure-point handhold. Hughes sprang back into action. Peter Greenaway swung over on his crane as well. "What's the most expensive thing on the menu, boy?"

"I . . . I dunno aaaaaaagggh. The Beef Wellington at five hundred and . . . aaaaaghhh!"

"We'll take twenty, with house wine then. Cut!"

"As I was saying, girls," Brett beamed on his way back to the table, "I really think you should consider skipping this benefit tonight."

"Homophobe!" yelled Pat.

"Be that as it may, these sorts of benefits are real downers, to be quite frank. I was over there already—the entire dance floor is covered by a quilt. It looks really slow. Please Starlight," he said, pushing Pat off the stage, "there's an important matter we need to discuss."

"I have no idea what sort of health insurance she has."

"No, no Starlight. Look, you simply can't go to the benefit tonight."

"We've been over this," she fumed, angry at the legal interference that so often complicates the artist's task.

"Not really," he said, rising to welcome two Japanese businessmen to the table. "Starlight, I'd like you to meet two publishing lawyer friends of mine. Now, according to these fellas, we'd be coming dangerously close to copyright infringement if you even go near that benefit tonight. Of course, meeting and dancing with me there is completely out of the question."

"What do you mean, copyright?"

"You don't need to know. The important thing is that we all agree you aren't going to that benefit. Now we've found a nice young man we're sure will show you a good time. All we need is for you to sign this legally binding statement saying, basically, that you'll be a good sport about the whole thing."

"Go to hell, Brett Butler," she screamed, "and take your accountants with you."

"Starlight, I was really hoping it wouldn't come to this." Brett motioned to the Japanese man nearest him, who rose, bowed to Starlight, and headed off into the crowd. Moments later, a short, balding Frenchman with a heavy accent appeared at their table.

"You are a dancer," he asserted.

"No," Starlight replied.

"But please there is no reason to be shy," he said. "I myself am a fantastic dancer."

Starlight moaned.

"I have credit," he proclaimed, brandishing a worn Gold Card at the assembled diners. "Credit is like sex, the smooth insertion of the card, the push and pull of the impressing device, the indelible impression it makes on the object of love."

Starlight looked from side to side, but could see no escape.

"Come with me," the Frenchman said, extending his hand. "I am a champion of lovemaking, and too often must do it alone."

"I'm not so sure about this," Starlight replied.

"Such a stupid, graceless girl," he replied. "I see you have a lot to learn. And I will be your teacher."

The copyright lawyers breathed a sigh of relief.

36

Chapter
SIX

And in the tiny mountain village of Ozarkania, there is general agreement as to the cause of the crisis. Mountain Man Bill explains:
Goddam paper money. Never trusted it. Fluoridated water, never drank it. Communists in the government, niggers in the woodpile, Jews in the banks, women in the kitchen. Never had a goddam thing to say to any of 'em. We may not look like honest people or good people mister, and truth is we ain't. But we got solid gold money, and you ain't got a goddam thing . . .

As a child I heard it with misgivings: the bulging pocket makes the easy life. And in the eastern United States, the inherent fallacy of this saying was being proved beyond a doubt. From Brett Butler's corner office in Rockefeller Center, Starlight O'Hara watched the gathering crowds rushing forward, moving back, stepping to the side as another window opened above them and another investment banker hurtled toward the pavement. As in all things, the difference between old and new money was clearly visible. Whether this was due to upbringing or merely a difference in the ballistic properties of Brooks Brothers and Armani, Starlight could not say, but its effects were plainly visible to all below.

Inside the office, frantic crash-helmeted figures clustered around the ticker-tape machine in the center of the trading department. "Freddie, bring her up!" one screamed. "Red switch, negative!" cried another. It was all very confusing.

"Brett, what on earth do they mean?" Starlight asked the one calm figure in the sea of mewling brokers.

"Something good happened," Brett responded.

"Oh! What?"

"I turned off the stock ticker. By the time they figure out how to turn it on again, my sell orders will have gone through."

"Isn't that immoral?"

"The way I see it," Brett explained, "I'm saving lives here. If you don't believe me, take a look at the foreign currency desk."

Starlight walked over to the one desolate corner of the office, Brett following close behind her. "I left their ticker on," Brett explained. "They fell in the line of duty."

The noise from the crowd below wafted in from the open window behind them. They walked over and cautiously looked outside. Another number went up on a huge tote board in the midst of the crowd.

"You're winning!" Starlight exclaimed.

"I wouldn't have paid their salaries anyway," Brett

said sadly. "Now get away from that window—I don't want you giving the rest of them any ideas."

Moving uncertainly away from the window, Starlight's heart went out to Brett and the brave young men who worked for him. So handsome in their pin-striped suits and Burberry ties, their polished backhands and Gucci attaché cases. Starlight remembered the morning they had left, a parade of German automobiles headed toward the Connecticut Turnpike while the entire female population of Scarsdale stood on the curb, Amex cards held high in salute. It seemed incredible that the seething mass of haggard faces and greasy hair in front of her was composed of the very same men, brothers, husbands, fathers, who had left town only a week before.

"What happened to all the money?" Starlight asked.

"It never really existed," Brett explained. "The dollar value of stocks was merely a reflection of societally held beliefs about the value of the assets they represented." Brett smiled and patted his pocket. "At least that's what I plan to tell the IRS."

"So if the money never existed," Starlight asked, "why is everyone so upset?"

"Because they thought it existed," Brett explained. "They bought coats with that money, they bought summer houses, they charged boats. Now the money's gone but they still have to pay."

"With what?" asked Starlight.

Brett gestured toward the window. "I wish I knew," he sighed. "A lot of my margin customers are behind on their payments."

"What happens to those people?" Starlight asked.

An alert young stockbroker came charging across the room toward the ticker-tape machine. "Close that damn

39

window!" Brett yelled to Starlight, who responded swiftly. The broker crashed headfirst through the plate glass and cartwheeled to the street below. The crowd let out a resounding cheer. Brett turned on his employees.

"You see?" he yelled. "You see? Is that the way you want to go?" The brokers mumbled uncertainly amongst themselves.

"Those are sharks out there! They want your blood! Are you going to give it to them?" The brokers began advancing toward the window.

"Jamie!" Brett said, picking out a young blond broker in the front of the crowd.

"Yes, sir."

"Your grandfather threw himself out a window in twenty-nine, right?"

"Yes, sir."

"But things got better, right? Your father made back all the money during the Korean War."

"He was in soybeans when the Cuban Missile Crisis hit, sir. He put a bullet through his head."

Brett smiled. "Where did he do it?"

"In the garage, sir."

"In other words he died at home with his family," Brett announced triumphantly.

"Mom had already divorced him by the time the market fell," Jamie answered. "I was the only one at home."

"And haven't you learned a lesson from all of this?"

"What sir?"

"That death is always ridiculous," Brett answered. "Killing other people may solve problems but killing yourself never does, unless the problems belong to someone else. And killing yourself because of someone else's problems is just about the stupidest thing I've ever heard. Now get back to work, all of you."

Never before had the sheer height of finance brought such pleasure to so many.

Brett sat down in one of the empty chairs near the tele-type machines, only to be jolted from his seat by a thundering bass voice that tore through the fragile calm of the trading floor like Herschel Walker through the Jets' defensive line.

"Butler!" roared the voice. "Look upon your works and despair, for the day of reckoning is upon you!"

The bearer of these extraordinary tidings made his way across the floor, preceeded by the even more extraordinary wooden club he employed as a cane. "The fool killer, Butler," the man pronounced, raising the club above his head and falling to the floor. "Woe to the fools!" he screamed, scrambling once again to a more or less upright position. "Woe to the fools, because their bills have finally come due."

"Indulging yourself so early in the morning, Doc Mead?" Brett asked.

"Morning?" the doctor screamed. "Way I see it Butler, it's high noon. You and me are headed for a showdown."

"It's ten A.M.," Brett replied, "and you seem ill-prepared for physical conflict with any of God's creatures."

Doc Mead pursed his lips and furrowed his brow. "I'm a doctor of medicine. I diagnose the ill, comfort the sick, and punish the disease. The way I see it . . ."

"I didn't know things were that serious," Brett began, a surprised grin on his face. "This society has been sick from the beginning. In our two-hundred-year history as a nation, we have made exactly two contributions to world culture—Paul Simon and Art Garfunkel, and they won't

41

even sing together anymore. God gave us William Faulkner: we made him write Hollywood movies. God gave us amber fields of grain: we make Wonder Bread. America has always been a nation of Americans: lazy, greedy bigots who would sell their birthright for a chili dog. All I do is take two percent off the top of the deal."

Doc Mead raised his stick above his head and shook it. "Once upon a time, this town was an honest town. You could—"

"Your fantasies of a kinder, gentler metropolis are appealing but completely untrue," Brett laughed. "I grew up in New York, and the city has grown with me. When I was a boy, a subway token was harder to come by than a season's subscription to the Metropoltian Opera, and twice as expensive. There were open holes in the sidewalks, and people fell in them and died so often it never made the news—it was just something you saw when you walked down the street. Clothes were a luxury only the rich could afford. Now everyone wears them. Things may be bad now but take it from me—they were worse before."

Doc Mead grew red in the face and shook his cane perilously close to Brett Butler's head. "Greed!" he yelled. "Avarice! Fancy suits and two-hundred-dollar ties! Benedict Arnold sold—"

"Maybe it's time we took another look at Benedict Arnold," Brett eagerly suggested. "He had access to information, and he used that information to make a profit for himself. At the same time, he opened up a narrowly funded institution to a great commitment of foreign resources that otherwise would have stayed at home."

"The institution of which you speak," Doc Mead replied, "was an American fortress. The foreign resources were British soldiers. Benedict Arnold betrayed his country for profit, and so have you."

"Well," said Brett, "that certainly wasn't the way Milton Friedman told the story. Boys!"

Two flannel-suited thugs pinned the doctor's arms to the top of his head and carried him away.

"Well, things seem to have settled down a little over here," Brett said, smartly clicking his heels. "Why don't we take a little stroll over to my office. If my calculations are correct, it should be about twice its former size."

The scene in Doc Mead's office was a psychiatrist's nightmare, and Starlight immediately regretted her rash scheduling of a midday appointment. Hundreds of business-suited brokers were crammed into every available inch of waiting-room space, credit cards expired, jobs lost, unable to afford the hourly rates. But even here, in the very depths of some uncharted circle of hell, the old ways continued to assert themselves.

"Tom Boddicker?" a voice yelled above the din. "My God! St. Paul's right?" Another voice screamed.

"You were in my sister's class, Amy Van Horne."

"Woaah," Tom yelled back. "Is that you, Skipster?"

"Yep. Backsies dude?" Skip asked. "I'm running way behind here."

"No problem!" Tom happily exclaimed, but it was drowned out by half-a-dozen competing claimants.

"Listen up!" Doc Mead roared, storming into the room. "There will be no use of prep school connections, no calling upon family ties or silly childhood nicknames for a better place in line. Those days are over, and you had better all get used to it, understand?" His patients looked chastened. "Anyone here take junior year abroad at the University of Tokyo?" Doc Mead asked. Not a hand was raised in response.

"Then I also feel completely justified in stating that wherever you went to college doesn't make a damn bit of difference anymore. The world has changed. For most of you, it will be an unrecognizable place, a place without maids, a place without year-end stock option bonuses, a place where nicknames like like Puff and Boops are best kept to yourselves. Some of you will have to put on uniforms and dish out junk food to anyone who asks for it, a job not entirely different from the ones you held before. You will be thrown together with people from all walks of life, some of whom never went to college.

"Think of it as an Outward Bound experience," he concluded, "except no one will make you eat Patagonia trail mix and no one will come and pick you up in a La Guardia–bound helicopter at the end of the week."

"What is it called?" one eager flaxen-haired broker demanded to know.

"Reality," Doc Mead responded. "Chances are, you'll be seeing a lot of it from now on."

Chapter
SEVEN

CHRISTMAS was my favorite holiday as a child. Only
then would my parents leave me alone in the house, all
the better to celebrate the holiday with those they loved.
I never minded, though. With some tongue sandwiches
in the refrigerator and a stack of movies by the VCR, I
had myself a hell of a time.

This Christmas season approached to find the U.S. financial sector in anything but a festive mood. The hours
of phone work and frequent flyer miles logged by
Hashley and countless others somehow lacked the romance and mystery they once held. As a topic of dinner
table conversation, high finance had all but disappeared.
No one wanted to be put off their food by talk of the
endless sea of bright young recent graduates being forced
to join the Peace Corps or seek employment in the entertainment industry.

When a rat lies dying on a lab-cage floor, healthier rats

will pretend it isn't there. Brokers let go shortly before the holidays were no longer received in the homes of those still employed. And when the entire trading wing at Sony Wilkes Brothers O'Hara protested that their holiday bonuses would not cover the cost of a single Nintendo cartridge, Hashley and the others turned away, knowing that there but for the grace of seniority, nepotism, and family planning went they.

Christmas dinner at Aunt Pat's was a subdued affair.

When Hashley entered, Melody in tow, Starlight was hit with the sudden realization that something about him had changed, something rooted so deep in his battered psyche that its most obvious symptom had eluded her. Yes, he still dressed the same, and yes, he still looked around continually for a place to lie down, but he was no longer trying to get away. He'd come to his senses at last! He would run no further from the feelings he harbored deep inside; he was trying to tell her he was ready, ready for love.

"Perhaps," he said, clearing his throat and struggling to his feet, "perhaps we could watch TV . . ."

"Yes! Yes! I thought you'd never ask," she gasped, moving toward him with outstretched arms.

"Such the hostess tonight, Starlight," he said, handing her his midnight-blue cashmere overcoat and Hermès scarf and proceeding into the den, "I'll get the telly warmed up."

Telly warmed up! He was toying with her, teasing her just as she had long imagined and prayed he would. She threw his wraps on the closet floor and ran into the den, only to find him fast asleep on the divan, one more victim of the NFL playoffs.

"Wake up! Wake up, damn you and give me what you promised!"

46

His eyes fluttered and then, with difficulty, fluttered open.

"I . . . I'm terribly sorry, Starlight," he said, smiling weakly and handing her a thin, gift-wrapped package. "Where are my manners? Merry Christmas."

Flustered and barely able to keep her tormented yearnings in tow, she opened the present with her teeth, slowly and sensuously until he began to nod off.

"Why, Hashley—five thousand shares of Sony—how . . . sweet."

"They're preferred," he yawned, rubbing his eyes.

"Oh, definitely, if you ask me. But you know I can't be bought—I'm independently wealthy."

"Well, Starlight, it's just that you'd be surprised at the number of people in this country who believe they're wealthier than they actually are. Why, we've both heard the stories of trust funds drying up. Money is always the first thing to go in romantic melodrama. P-Please," he gasped, "put those away."

"You're so caring, Hashley, so giving," said Starlight, continuing to unbutton her blouse, "but you don't know how to take."

"P-Perhaps you could give me my present now, and then we'll call it even . . ."

Had she been rash? Perhaps she had hurt his feelings, insulted him by not giving him his present the minute he walked in the door. How was he to know that she still cared for him when he had waited so long with no hint of her having gotten him anything?

"The *Book of Mormon*. How . . . positively charming. You know how fascinated I am with religious cults. Where on earth did you find it?"

"Oh, really, it doesn't compare to your present. I still feel as if I owe you something."

"Nonsense—you know the value of a book can't be measured, Starlight."

"It cost nineteen ninety-five. How much are those certificates worth?"

"Really, Starlight—it's not right, talking about such things."

"How much? They're mine, aren't they? I have a right to know."

"S-Several thousand, I'm not sure. It changes you know."

"In any case," she said, stepping out of her green DKNY miniskirt and moving toward him, "we are left with a clear discrepancy of several thousand dollars. Anywhere else in this city that would entitle you to quite a night." Those who think Starlight forward are correct, but this I know for certain: they have never been alone on Christmas Eve.

In the bathroom, Starlight sat on the bowl while her mind swirled. Was she dreaming, or had that not been quite the disaster she thought it had been? Normally, this was exactly the kind of thing that could ruin one's reputation, but Melody had not seemed to mind. Perhaps Melody was getting too fat to satisfy him. She had read about this sort of thing every month in *Cosmopolitan* for as long as she could remember, and one recommended cure was a surrogate lover. Did Melody read *Cosmopolitan* too?

Moments later, Starlight looked around the table at the newly arrived guests, so proper in their starched white Giuliano Fujiwara shirts and Mary McFadden fortuny pleats. Although they had not been formally introduced, she felt an immediate kinship with them, so elegant, so strange, so Southern. The woman on her left asked for the salt.

"Thank you, whoever you are," she sighed as Starlight handed her the pepper as well. "I've always depended upon the kindness of strangers."

"Doesn't look like they've been too kind lately," Starlight offered sympathetically, making eyes at Hashley across the table.

"I wish I had created someone memorable to participate in this conversation," sighed a pale, bespectacled woman sitting to their left.

"What Flannery is referring to," interjected Hashley, "is Melody's pregnancy. We made the announcement while you were in the bathroom. Isn't it wonderful news?"

Starlight glared contemptuously at the expectant couple and attempted to kick Hashley beneath the table.

"Ouch!" offered a slender woman in her midforties. "Perhaps you should consider returning home now, Starlight. I found that returning to your ancestral home at a time like this can be the beginning of a profound journey to self-awareness."

"You can't go home again," said a depressed-looking young man who appeared to have been in New York for a while.

"You bite your tongues," bellowed a huge woman who appeared to be feeding some kind of pet underneath the table, "or I'll damn well rip 'em out of your heads and feed 'em to Lymon!"

"Not mine, you old sow," coughed a fat old geezer with a white goatee. "Ain't nothin the matter with me. I ain't plannin' on dying for a good long while, don't you worry."

"Please, Colonel Sanders," said a forlorn young man wearing a Harvard tie. "You'll frighten Boo with all this morbid conversation."

"The name's Pollit. And maybe that's what you boys need—a little shock, a little reminder to get the adrenaline working again." He grabbed the candelabra and shoved it in Boo's face.

"Ugh!" screamed Boo, falling backward in his chair, away from the flame.

"See what I mean?" screamed Big Daddy triumphantly. "He chose to protect himself, to embarrass himself rather than burn. He chose life, which is more than I can say for most of you."

"Excuse me," said Binx, a well-dressed man with an easy manner, "but this all reminds me of a movie I once saw. Actually, I must have seen it several times over the years . . . or was it several movies, each of which I've seen only once? I suppose it doesn't matter, ultimately. Anyone up for *Rocky Horror* later on?"

"More talk, dammit!" bellowed Pat. "More tempestuous Southern women and their dessicated male counterparts! And more wine!"

"Really, Pat," said Hashley, "I think we've all had enough, really."

"I'm afraid that was the last, Miss Pat," said Flannery.

"Of the Cadet?" she gasped in disbelief.

"Of the genre."

Everyone at the table was sobered by the announcement. The genre was the last thing Pat had left. Aside from the trusts, the properties, and the money those nice Japanese men had paid her recently for her some dusty old shares she had lying around, she was ruined.

Mercifully, the extreme shock, the late hour, and a

feeling very much like that of a heavy hand pressing down on her cranium caused her to fall face forward into the plum pudding. Embarrassed for the old woman, the guests departed, intending never to call again.

"Starlight," said Hashley later, when the two of them were alone. "This is so very hard for me . . ."

"What, Hashley? What is it?"

"I . . . that is . . . we would like to have relations with you. No strings attached, you understand . . ."

It was more than she had dared dream for! Hashley wanting her to bear his offspring! It was a perfect match, and his use of the royal "we" had been positively the most charming thing she had ever heard in her entire life. As if to answer, she fell into his arms, and, calling upon all his reserves, he carried her into the guest room. She was far too drunk to walk there on her own.

I'll have to remember to ask Doc Mead about that one, she thought the next morning as she headed for the bathroom in search of a nonaspirin analgesic. In the hallway, she met Hashley, dressed in the same suit he had worn to dinner.

"Good morning, Starlight. Love to stay and chat, but I've got to get back to the front, if you know what I mean."

"I'm sorry, I see I must have spilled wine on your tie."

"Do you like it? It was a gift from Melody—the whole outfit was, you know. She's awfully fond of you, Starlight."

"I'll pay to have it cleaned, if that's what you're getting at."

"Starlight, darling—don't be silly."

"Like I was last night?"

"Y-You weren't silly. You were . . . fabulous, Starlight, and you know how awfully fond of you Melody is—"

"What about Melody?"

"I . . . want you to take care of her, Starlight. It's very important to me, to both of us. I want things to be the way they were . . . last night, do you understand."

"Say no more, my darling, she smoldered conspiratorially as he blew her a kiss. It was so simple, why had it not occurred to her? It was important to them, to their love, that Melody be terminated, with extreme prejudice, immediately. No love of their magnitude, of their power, could reach its true potential with an outsider in the way. And as they say in the West, extremism in the pursuit of love is no vice.

"Tradition," shouted Brett as he and Yamamoto skated around the rink at Rockefeller Center, hand in hand. "I love traditions. Christmas, weddings, Hanukkah. Even our little talks. Traditions are felled right and left by the inexorable march of time. We have a responsibility, each and every one of us, to continue and strengthen those which have somehow survived."

Yamamoto, in a festive mood, refused to answer.

Chapter
EIGHT

"IT'S so beautiful!" exclaimed Melody as Starlight returned from a stroll down Fifth Avenue. "It's kicking inside me."

She lay on the couch, her thin, waifish body bloated beyond recognition.

"Think of pleasant things," Starlight soothingly recommended. "Think of Bob Dylan." Melody purred softly. "Yes, Bob Dylan is standing right next to you, with his guitar and a battered fedora, singing all your favorite songs from the *Infidels* album."

"Arrgh!" Melody screamed, her head whipping back and forth.

"Hush, hush, my darling," Starlight said, reaching down and squeezing Melody's hand. "You don't want to get upset and lose the baby. Hashley will divorce you if that happens."

"Yes, Bob Dylan is standing right next to you, with his guitar and a battered fedora, singing all your favorite songs from the *Infidels* album."

54

"Starlight, darling, you mustn't say such cruel things," Melody whimpered. "Hashley and I wanted to have this baby. He said it would be a combination of our best qualities."

"That's a Chia Pet, honey, not a person," Starlight barked. "Birth control was invented so that no man could force himself upon a woman and make her swell up like Judd Nelson's head." Starlight's eyes narrowed. "If I were you, I'd report it to the police."

"Report what?" Melody asked.

"This disgusting rape," Starlight answered. "I'm sure you're partly to blame, but you do have to live with the consequences."

Melody recoiled in horror. "Starlight, I told you, we're having this baby out of love."

"I'm sorry, Melody. It's simply too disgusting for me to think about it any other way. Now, if you'll—"

Starlight was interrupted by a high-pitched shriek from the couch. "Omigod!" Melody cried. "The contractions are starting. Get a bowl of hot water and—aaaugh!"

"Love to help you out," Starlight said, moving toward the door, "but what if something went wrong? I'd be liable."

"Get Ramie then!" Melody yelped. "Doesn't she have a nursing degree or something? Starlight go quick!"

Reluctantly, Starlight shuffled out and returned a few minutes later with Ramie.

"I done tol' you Miss Starlight," Ramie said, "I doan' know a thing 'bout birfin' babies."

"Speak like a normal person," Melody hissed. "We're quite aware that you're colored."

Ramie smiled and sat down on the bed next to Melody. "I hopes he shred you like tissue paper," she said warmly.

At this Melody cried even harder. "I voted for Jesse Jackson in the primary. I give to the NAACP. We pay our maid twice what's fair. Please!"

"Slabes done gib birf to they babies in the fiel'. Ain' no reason why you cain't birf yo'se on the couch."

"Melody," Starlight interjected. "I'm sure Ramie would help if she could. Don't take it so personal."

Ramie shot Starlight an evil glance and the accent disappeared. "I graduated at the top of my class at Albert Einstein College of Medicine. But I didn't become a doctor to bring white babies into this world to cheat on their taxes and vote Republican. Maybe this child will grow up and become a kind person with a highly developed social conscience, but from where I sit, the odds don't look too good." And with that, Ramie walked into the next room to watch TV.

A soft cry came from the direction of the bed.

"Shut up, Melody," Starlight snapped, as the cry became a slow gurgling noise. "I said, shut up."

Infuriated at this reckless disregard of her explicit instructions, Starlight turned around only to find Melody incapable of responding. A human infant was crawling across Melody's abdomen, attached to her by a kind of tether. Starlight screamed and ran into the kitchen, returning seconds later with a knife. She lashed out at the tether just as Melody was gaining consciousness.

"Thank you, Starlight," she said softly, cradling her newborn child in her arms. "Isn't he beautiful?"

"And now I suppose you're going to lick him clean," Starlight said, disgusted. "This is enough to make anyone sick. Now get up and start packing. Delivering a baby is backbreaking work. It's time for a vacation—Palm

56

Springs maybe, or Martinique. We'll all go."

"But how will we get to the airport?" Melody asked.

"Brett," Starlight said aloud. After all, Brett was the only person they knew whose BMW convertible hadn't been repossessed. "Go find Brett," she told Melody. "He'll give us a ride."

Melody took three tentative steps toward the door, but her knees buckled and she sat quickly down on the sofa. "Starlight, I can't," she said. "I can't make it to Nell's."

"You wouldn't say that if they had an open bar," Starlight crossly replied. Realizing it was up to her to get them out of town, she took the elevator down, proceeded to a pay phone outside, and dialed Brett's private extension.

Brett answered the phone with a gruff "Hello."

"I was wondering if I could come visit you now," Starlight said coyly. "I was also wondering if you could give us a ride to the airport."

"Why do you need to visit me here if you want me to take you to the airport?" Brett inquired, clearly miffed.

"My point exactly."

"Nice try. But this is real life, not pulp fiction, and the hero doesn't always come to the rescue."

Brett returned to his table, where Yamamoto sat waiting.

"And what shall we discuss today, my friend?"

"The death of responsibility," Brett grunted.

"Love to," said Yamamoto, rising and bowing, "but I really do have to run. Sorry about the check, old man. Next time, my treat."

57

*   *   *

A smiling security guard greeted Starlight, Melody, and Ramie at the sliding doors to the North Terminal. "Kindly step away from the doors," he requested. "Please step away."

"Isn't there anyone to help us with our bags?" Starlight asked, affronted.

The guard stared right through her. "Mr. Lorenzo doesn't like people standing so close to the doors," he said, reaching for his belt.

"But—" Starlight began, but she was immediately cut off by a burst of automatic weapons fired from hip level. The guard's placid expression remained unchanged.

"Please get away from the doors," he said. The trio complied immediately, only to be accosted by a man in the tattered remains of a Brooks Brothers 345 suit, his tie clip grasping at one of many empty buttonholes on his Turnbull and Asser shirt. "Do you have two thousand miles you can spare?" he asked. "I need to be in Denver for a very important meeting, and I need two thousand miles."

"Put it on American Express," Starlight suggested.

"They don't take credit cards anymore," the man said. "Cash either. That's why we're all stuck here," he said, motioning toward the droves of tattered business travelers. "See that one," he asked, pointing to a particularly sad-looking man in a crushed J. Press blazer. "Two hundred more miles and he'd be Shuttle Plus. And until he gets there, he stays here, with the rest of us."

"He can't fly until he gets the miles," Starlight said slowly. "But without the miles he can't leave the waiting room. He'll never get out—it's awful!"

"That's the beauty of the system!" the man replied,

suddenly animated. "Only the deserving get to fly. Those who've flown the most miles get to fly the most! I should have done the Chase Manhattan Air plan. I hear if you have leftover miles after your flight, you can trade them in for the developing nation of your choice."

The man continued. "I think we'll be able to tell future generations how we watched the WASPs spend their last moments in an airport departure lounge, suits ripped, luggage lost, lucky to find a hot dog in the trash. Trains were the way WASPs got around. Trains allowed for the division of social classes—club car for us, cattle car for everyone else. The airplane was the death of the class system, although few recognized it at the time. On an airplane, everyone is equal. Business Class, Clipper Class, Economy—the names are different but the food is the same and no one has any room to stretch out their feet, let alone relax at a card table."

Starlight walked out of the airport bathroom still buttoning her blouse. It wasn't particularly enjoyable, but Starlight had managed to exchange the only currency she had left for four frequent flyer vouchers.

As they boarded the flight, Melody looked wistfully back at the men's room. The vacation itself was uneventful.

Chapter
NINE

"JUST a few more blocks," said Starlight from the backseat.

"For to tote the weary load," hummed the driver, under his breath.

They topped the rise and before them lay Scarsdale as they had never imagined it. Everywhere, real estate signs dotted the lawns, though not a single one said Sold. As they drew closer, Starlight understood for the first time what it must be like to come from a poor neighborhood—hardly a tennis court had been swept in days, most of the pools had been left unchlorinated, and not a single hedge was properly manicured.

"Look like dey fired de help already," said Ramie, pouting. "No surprise—dey always de first to go."

"Well, it's certainly no wonder, considering the awful job they've been doing," snapped Starlight. "Why, just look at Mrs. Merriwether's BMW—it hasn't been waxed in weeks, and that garage door could use a coat of paint if I'm a week old."

"Johnny's a week old!" exclaimed Melody, brushing Starlight's thigh lightly.

"Will you shut up about that little monster of yours?" shrieked Starlight, pushing her away and frightening the baby.

As she slid down on the seat and grabbed the baby's blanket for cover, Starlight realized that none of her fellow travelers was at all mindful of how easily this journey could end in disaster if they were spotted. Why, what if Emmy Slandery heard that Starlight O'Hara Hamilton had been seen riding home in a common taxi cab? She'd be ruined—didn't they understand? Didn't they care?

She could sense that something was amiss the instant the cab turned onto the cedar-canopied road. No matter how thickly the branches intertwined they had never before cast the drive in such blackness. Were her tired globes deceiving her, or was Tarot no longer there? The paisley walls, the windows fluttering with tie-dyed curtains—did they lie ahead in the gloom?

"Oh, Tarot! My home!" she screamed as the cab came to a halt. "Gone, all gone."

"Oh, for shame," said Ramie, turning around in her seat. "Pull that rag off your head and pay the man."

As Starlight handed the driver her American Express Platinum Card and looked out over the yard, she wished Tarot had not been there after all, for nothing in the rest of the neighborhood could have prepared her for what she saw. Apparently deserted, the house was almost entirely surrounded by some variety of weed higher than their heads and stretching as far as the eye could see.

Ramie laughed, "You can't pay a cabbie with a credit card."

Starlight was confused. How was one supposed to pay, then? For the first time in her life, she found herself at a complete loss for what to do next. Melody certainly had no money, and it just wouldn't be right asking Ramie to pay. Perhaps if they offered him the baby . . .

"It's no problem, ma'am," he said, handing her card back, "I'll accept payment in kind."

The driver got out of the car and Starlight consigned herself to her fate as he stuffed the trunk and floorboards of the cab with as much of the foliage as would inconspicuously fit and drove away at a breakneck speed.

Inside, Starlight stood in the hallway and struggled to detect some sign of life. "Hello? Is anyone home?" Her heart leapt for joy when she heard no answer. If no one was living here now, then Tarot was hers. But even as she imagined the Laura Ashley wallpaper everywhere, a dim flickering light from the living room caught her eye. At first she could make out very little, as the one dying jasmine-scented candle in the room provided scant illumination. But as she moved closer and her eyes adjusted, she became aware of a distinctly human shape laid out, unmoving, on the coffee table.

"Daddy? Is that you?" she called softly, but there came no reply. Lighting another candle, she realized with a gasp who it was. That face—it had to be, but how? "Mother!"

Her mind reeling, Starlight struggled for some explanation. Her mother had been dead for several years, but this corpse was fresh.

"Boo!" it said.

Starlight let out a blood-curdling scream and involuntarily jumped several feet into the air. When she landed, the corpse was laughing.

"Sioux-Ellen!"

"Gotcha, didn't I?" she mumbled, scratching the side of her face weakly.

"Did not."

"Did too."

"Where's Daddy? Where's Chamois?"

"Food for thought, huh—both of 'em missing at the same time?"

"What are you doing here, Sioux-Ellen?"

"The band broke up. I live here now."

"You are not painting swastikas all over your bedroom again, if that's what you mean."

"I live here . . ." she chuckled, groping about clumsily for another syringe. "Here on the coffee table and you'd better get used to it."

Starlight wondered how on earth she was going to cope.

"Starlight?" It was that horrid little Melody, with Ramie fast on her heels. "We were getting cold. What's wrong with Sioux-Ellen? Is she OK? Are those syringes on the floor?"

"Oh, fiddle-dee-dee!" said Starlight, cool and graceful with her family reputation on the line. "Her blood sugar is as normal as yours or mine. Now, let's stop all this senseless gossiping and get some sleep."

What makes a man great? Is it something in the air? The water he drinks? Is it fate, or the ability to conquer that fickle mistress? Over the next few weeks, Starlight had her hands full trying to make Tarot the dream home she knew it could be. Day after day she dialed number after number—getting the electricity turned back on, having the laundry picked up, ordering new furniture.

She soon lost count of how many nails she'd broken in the dialing process, and often her fingertips ached so badly at night that she could barely operate the remote.

The local free-lance horticulturist's advice still burning in her ears, Starlight searched for her father one morning and found him kneeling by the side of the indoor pool, stark naked in a pair of green Converse high-tops.

"Daddy—what are you putting in the pool? Is that chlorine?"

"It's nothing, man. Just an old dude and his toys."

"What's in those vials? What are you doing there?"

"Having a few buddies over this evening, man; stay out of the pool if you don't want to trip."

"Unlike you and your friends, I have no trouble keeping my balance, thank you very much."

"Hey man, that's what it's all about," he mused, diving in without removing his sneakers.

"Daddy," she said when he resurfaced. "We need to talk."

"It's true, man," he agreed, treading water and spinning around in an attempt to mix the contents of the pool. "Without speech, mankind would still be in the dark ages."

"I had a man come out and look at the gardens this morning. At first he tried to say all that overgrowth was grass, but I told him he was flat wrong—no grass I'd ever seen had stems and leaves like that. Then he said 'weed,' and I told him I didn't care how innocently it had started, because God knows how quickly they grow. I told him the only thing I was interested in was getting rid of them, and he offered to introduce me to a couple of his friends.

"Can you imagine that? There I was right in the middle of the most embarrassing situation in the world and all he can think about is fixing me up with his sleazy friends. I fired him then and there, but do you know he had the nerve to charge me several times his normal rate to keep his mouth closed? Daddy—you're not listening to me!"

She had guessed correctly, for Jerry was now floating at the bottom of the pool.

"How many was that?" he asked, coming to the surface and gasping for air.

"How many what?"

"Laps, man."

"Zero. You weren't really moving."

"Wow. Used to be able to do a lot more than that, man."

"Daddy, I realize this may come as a shock to you, but I'm going to set fire to the gardens this afternoon; I'm sorry. I know how much they've meant to you, but you've really let them go to pot lately and I've just got to do something about it before stories start to circulate."

As Jerry floated on his back and stared blankly at the tiled ceiling, Starlight wondered why he was not responding in any way to the news, why he was no longer blinking, why his legs were twitching like that.

"Daddy! Daddy, are you alright? Did you hear what I said?"

As if in response, the twitching ceased and he began to drift away across the water, smiling.

"Look at that disgusting creature" said Yamamoto, standing at the corner of Ashbury and Haight Streets in San Francisco, "selling drugs to kids."

Starlight had guessed correctly, for Jerry was now
floating at the bottom of the pool.

"Drugs are a plague," said Butler.

"A curse," agreed Yamamoto.

"No substitute for a proper education."

"Certainly not," mused Yamamoto, staring straight into the sun, "but they sure do get you high."

Later that day, after thoroughly spraying the gardens with kerosene and sending Melody in with a Bic lighter, Starlight felt she was truly in control of her own destiny for the first time in her short, pampered life. She knew now that one truly did make one's own karma, and resolved to crush anyone who stood in the way of her making hers.

The only remaining threat to Starlight's supremacy at Tarot was Chamois, but the very thought of a confrontation with the crafty old servant made her shiver. Chamois no longer seemed to have any interest whatsoever in the day-to-day doings of Tarot. She no longer cooked, even for herself, and Starlight was therefore saddled with the extra burden of ordering out several times a day. This made her fingertips all the sorer, but Chamois did not seem to care. God only knew what she was up to in there.

"Chamois?" she said, knocking lightly, "Can I speak with you?"

"Sho'," came the reply. "I kin hear you jus' fine from dere."

"I'd like to come in."

"Well, you cain't. Anythin' else you be wantin' to discuss wif ole Chamois, don' you hesibitate to come on back."

Frightened by the odd, sickly sweet green smoke that was beginning to fill the hallway, Starlight tried the door and found it unlocked.

"I'm sorry, Chamois," she said, walking in and closing the door behind her, "I feel . . . a bit dizzy."

"You always been dizzy," said Chamois, getting up and throwing both her windows open.

"Don't jump!" Starlight screamed.

"Ol' Chamois ain' goin' nowheres, she jes' lettin in de night air," she laughed, pointing at the pile of thousand-dollar bills on her bed. "You go right ahead an' jump ef you feels like it, but ole Chamois gots plenty to keeps her alibe."

"Where on earth did that come from?"

"Dat is called money, an' it come from Chamois bein' safebly in bonds durin' de current financial crisis."

"Does this mean you're leaving us?"

"Ol' Chamois gots plenty of money an' a nice room. She gawna stick around, leas' till she evicted."

"I'm getting awfully hungry," Starlight confided.

"Eben de formably rich gots to pay dey bills," Chamois said. "Ain't a place in town gwine deliver here."

"What on earth do you mean, 'formerly rich'?"

"Yo' pa done poured ebry cent he had inta dat cash crop you burnin' in de backyard. De 'nishal cash-outlay happ'n a while ago, but afta dem Japonaise persons bought up his comp'ny, he done spent ebry las' dime he had on fertilizer. You busted."

Something broke deep within Starlight. She could do without some of the comforts she had grown accustomed to, but being wealthy was not one of them. Rising unsteadily, she raced through the mind-numbing haze that now filled the room, down the staircase and out onto the back patio, fully unprepared for what she would find there.

Well-lit by the inferno in the gardens, hundreds of people just like her father were dancing fluidly in those parts of the yard not directly on fire. Starlight was near panic when she spotted a tray of freshly baked brownies sitting on the poolside table.

"What's in those?" she demanded of the nearby dead-head dancing with Johnny.

"Hash, man. The little dude's mom made them."

It was more than she could bear! Melody alive, the money up in smoke, and the only food around made with common potatoes.

"Stop this!" she screamed, waving her arms at the dazed partiers on the patio. "You'll have to stop that dancing, put down whatever food you have in your hands, and leave it for me. I might not be able to get something in the morning, and I may want a little something before then anyway. I'm not asking you to leave anything you may have brought in with you, but—"

"Dude," laughed the deadhead, biting into one of the brownies as the crowd moved in to love bomb her. "No offense, but I think you should stay clear of the pool tonight."

Chapter
TEN

EVERY day the high-speed tour buses roared through Scarsdale, and every day clumps of For Sale signs disappeared from the overgrown lawns and unpainted facades, along with Maytag washer-dryers, baseball card collections, and framed diplomas from Harvard and Yale.

But Starlight refused to sell. Rolling pin and featherduster in hand, she continued her uphill battle to restore Tarot, if not to its former glory then at least to a place where she could set out an afternoon tray of Ritz crackers and Brie. This was a far different Starlight than the shallow, headstrong slip of a girl who once upon a time flirted with boys and played Marco Polo in the club pool. She was at peace with herself, a peace now shattered by the incessant ringing of the doorbell. Wearily, Starlight reloaded her Luger and opened the door.

A Japanese couple and a miniskirted real estate agent

stood waiting outside. "Hi, Starlight," the agent cooed. "Ready to give up?"

"Hell no," Starlight growled, but the couple had already slipped inside. Both the male and the female were over six feet tall, with a slight trace of Oxbridge in their voices.

"A charming example of Psychedelic Colonial," the man announced. "The beanbag Ralph Lauren couch is an especially piquant example of the genre, wouldn't you say?"

"Ooooh," the woman sighed. "Separate air-conditioning units in the windows!"

"A little Walden," the man chimed in. "So restful, so basic—it's straight out of the pages of *Town and Country*."

"Six million," the woman said, turning to Starlight.

Her husband was unable to contain himself. "Ten million dollars for your charming little home!"

Starlight stared at them, flabbergasted. "What?" she asked. "What are you doing in my house? Get out immediately."

The couple was taken aback, but only for an instant. "Twenty million then," the husband offered.

"No," Starlight answered. "This is my home. I had my first period on that beanbag. Bobby Post kissed me for a dollar under that apple tree. I'll never sell Tarot," she venomously proclaimed, "especially not to a foreigner."

"But to call us foreign is silly," the man answered, laughing. "I was an All-American first baseman at UCLA. I can quote large sections of *Leaves of Grass* from memory. I own all of Jackson Pollock's work. Come

71

on—I'll bet you can't even name the capitals of all fifty states."

"A true American doesn't have the slightest idea who his congressman is," Starlight retorted. "If MTV isn't good enough for you, why don't you go back to Poland or wherever it was you said you came from."

"But don't you see?" the man explained. "We're saving your culture from extinction. We love America too much to leave it in the hands of Americans."

Enraged, Starlight reached for her gun. "A typical American solution," the woman sneered. Starlight trained the pistol on her.

"That's exactly right," she said, and shot them both.

Melody bounded down the stairs.

"Take these two bodies and put them out with the trash," Starlight commanded. "They tried to take away our home." Meekly, Melody complied.

As Melody was dragging the last of Starlight's handiwork out the back door, Jerry burst in the front.

"Whoa," he yelled. "War's over, man!" He clutched Starlight to his breast, and raised a clenched fist in the air. "We brought the system to its knees, man—we made it do the chicken."

Starlight looked at him, bewildered. "What are you talking about?"

"The people are in the streets in Chicago!" he announced. "Our people! Let's see that lying Texan and the numbers boys in Defense send another fifty thousand boys to go die in the jungle, man!"

"What Texan?" Starlight asked.

"The one who shot Kennedy," Jerry replied. "Lyndon what's-his-name."

No sooner had Jerry gone outside to celebrate the disruption of the 1968 Democratic National Convention than the press, alerted by a real estate agent minus two of her more promising clients, began to call.

"Starlight O'Hara?" a voice asked.

"Yes," Starlight replied in her best Fairfield County Lockjaw.

"This is the *Wall Street Journal*. Is it true that you shot two Japanese investors for attempting to purchase your home?"

Starlight sighed. "Yes, I suppose it is. If the Fed can't be trusted to protect our economy, citizens must do what they can to protect their own investments."

"Um, how much did they offer."

"Their last offer was twenty million dollars," Starlight answered proudly. "I'd be damned if any descendant of Fitzhugh O'Hara and John Jacob Astor would sell a home that has hosted the Junior League Cotillion. The only *Register* those people understand is the kind in department stores."

"How many bedrooms does your house have?" CBS News inquired.

"Three."

"Hmm," CBS answered. "Twenty million dollars is a lot of money."

"To what do you owe your remarkable strength of will," *The New York Times* wanted to know.

"Early mornings rowing crew, a mandatory sport, and no boys in the dorms after lights out," Starlight replied.

"Do you think good breeding had anything to do with your decision?" asked *Vogue*.

"Definitely," Starlight answered. A legend was born. There wasn't a jury in the country that would convict her, and with the obligatory sale of her life story to *Peo-*

73

ple, Tarot would be restored to its former grandeur in no time at all.

"Violence," said Yamamoto as he and Brett stood before the Iwo Jima monument, "never solved anything."

"I beg to differ," laughed Butler, feeling patriotic. "Violence solved our little disagreement with your country quick enough."

"Be that as it may," Yamamoto responded, growing red in the face, "Violence is the coward's solution."

"The coward's solution is to surrender once you drop an atom bomb on his family."

"Only a coward would invent such a bomb."

"Are you calling Albert Schweitzer a coward?"

"Yes! Yes, I am!"

"I must disagree."

"On what grounds?"

"He did not invent the bomb."

A karate chop later, Brett had completely changed his position on Albert Schweitzer, father of the atomic bomb.

As the WASPs poured back into Scarsdale, the help poured out. Maids of twenty-five years, French au pairs, Salvadorean gardeners and their wives drove off with their heads held high. "Maybe you will come visit your husband's office some day, yes?" . . . "Have you heard the news—our Chiquita has been accepted at Exeter." The humiliation of the Old Guard was now complete.

One day, among the long line of the walking wounded who spent their days sitting in the driveway or playing Trivial Pursuit by the pool came Bubba Kennedy. Emaciated and possessed of a long flowing beard that he wore to make up for his early baldness, he was a terrifying vision—haggard, wan, a vision of what JFK might have become had he stuck with Jackie another ten years.

"I want Sioux-Ellen back," he begged Starlight late one afternoon. "I know I don't look like much, but then again, neither does she if memory serves."

Starlight's upper lip curled with unconcealed disdain. "Absolutely not," she replied.

Bubba recoiled in shock and surprise. "What's the problem? I'm a Kennedy aren't I?"

"Once trash, always trash," Starlight giggled. "If there's one thing this disaster has freed us from, it's having to read about the Kennedy children failing out of school or sleeping with talentless starlets. Camelot is over, dead and gone. I'll be damned if my sister is going to produce a passel of drug-addicted brats who can't even get a full page in *People*. Besides, she isn't living here these days."

Bubba nearly collapsed with grief. "Wh-where is she staying?"

"The Hazelden Clinic," Starlight responded triumphantly as Bubba took off down the driveway at a pace she found remarkable for someone of his size. "Perhaps you've heard of it."

Not long afterward, another visitor showed up in line for Jerry's Magic Stew. Starlight buckled at the knees when she recognized him. Hashley! said her heart, but a second glance told quite another story. In bright red pants and a shirt with no collar, a portfolio of Julian Schnabel prints under his arm, the pudgy figure before her could just as well have been a loud accountant from Great Neck buying modern painters as a hedge against inflation. He bore little resemblance to the narcoleptic

75

aesthete with a taste for the late Renaissance of Starlight's memory.

"War do terrible things to dose dat see it," commented Chamois. "Some lose dey libes, others lose dey minds, an' some lose dey aesthetic sensibility. Ol' Chamois neber seed a case dis bad, dough."

While Chamois attempted to explain to Starlight why men start wars and crack up afterward, an emotional reunion was taking place between Hashley and Melody.

"Hashley!"

"Darling," he said weakly, "Grand to see you."

"Give me those awful prints," Melody said, snatching the Schnabels from under his arm. "Now come upstairs and see the baby. I named him after your favorite painter—Gotti."

"Giotto," Hashley corrected her, but then stopped. "Oh what does it matter—everything is lost now."

"Would you like to lie down?" Melody asked compassionately.

"I'd like that very much," Hashley replied. "On second thought, do the O'Haras still have those Warhol silk screens in the living room?"

Melody shuddered inside, but remained calm. "Yes they do, dear," she answered.

The road back was going to be rocky.

Chapter
ELEVEN

IN a move that many are calling unparalleled, unprecedented, and highly unusual, Governor Mario Cuomo announced today a statewide luxury tax to raise funds desperately needed in the battle against homelessness:

Right on! We're finally gonna see some change for the better. Someone up there is listening . . .

Thank God somebody cares, you know. Sometimes, it's, like, nobody listens, but God bless Mario today, though . . .

Personally, I don't trust the guy . . .

In other news, religious leader Charles Manson is once again up for parole this month. If released, the former madman says he will embark upon a career in politics. Available polls show that—

"Turn it off!" screamed Starlight, "That face—I can't stand it! Turn it off!"

"It be ugly, but he might register 'publican, in which case you an' yo' friends will mos' likely see dat he pardoned an' 'lected to high office."

"You know perfectly well I'm talking about that horrible Emmy Slandery. Who let her on TV?"

"She white—why cain't she be on?"

"Because I own the damn thing, and I want it off!"

"Wasn't all dat long ago you could say dat 'bout ol' Chamois' head," Chamois sighed, holding the remote tightly.

"Oh . . . shoot!" said Starlight. "Why on earth you want to sit here and listen to that trash take credit for every good thing that happens is beyond me."

"You likes dis idea?"

"Who wouldn't? President Reagan said that the only way to get rid of a bad thing is to cut funding for it or tax it heavily. Cutting funds doesn't seem to be making those people go inside so maybe it is time to start taxing them."

"You misreadin' de sitiation," Chamois explained. "T'ain' de homeless dat gots to pay dis tax."

"What on earth are you trying to say?"

"I'se sayin' de tax on you, Missy Starlight."

It is the duty of every responsible citizen to pay taxes. But when taxes get too high, it is the duty of the citizen to protest. Paying for homeless people was taking things too far.

"Emmy Slandery just wants me to be as poor and embarrassed as she is," Starlight wailed.

"Seem to me she akshuly proud she don' come from money."

"Don't be ridiculous, Chamois. She just acts that way to save face, because deep down she knows no matter

78

how much her kind gains and our kind loses, her kind will always be genetically inferior. Don't you know anything about reverse psychology?"

"I knows dat ef you reversed yo'se de worl' be a betta place."

Perhaps there was some truth to what Chamois said. She had heard of those people so locked into one way of thinking that it crippled them permanently. Well, those people could just rot in hell for all she cared. She for one was not too high and mighty to admit there had been a serious flaw in her thinking. She had been spending her time and energy trying to figure out *why* Emmy had done this when the real question at hand was *how* to get her back.

Later that evening, as she crept downstairs to take her tray of s'mores out of the oven, Chamois heard Starlight on the phone to AP, UP, Reuters, the *Times,* the *Post,* and every local station but Emmy's, introducing herself each time as "Starlight O'Hara Hamilton, the front-yard vigilante," and inviting them all to attend a press conference at Tarot the following afternoon where an important announcement would be made. "And by the way," she said, "refreshments will be served—lots of them."

In her suite high atop the Scarsdale Hilton, Chamois flipped the channels on the twenty-four-inch color screen and looked for Emmy's. She had missed most of the local news lounging by the pool, but knew she was right on time for Emmy's "Last Laugh" segment, as she rarely missed it.

Finally tonight, you may remember a certain Scarsdale banking heiress who shot a Japanese couple last week.

Well, the front-yard vigilante is back in the news again, but this time all she's armed with is a questionable acquittal and a rather confused new cause . . .

On the videotape, Starlight stood behind an art-deco podium she had set up in the front yard and shuffled through an immense pile of notes. Far behind her, a long row of picnic tables with an immense amount of food piled on them were being visited by what appeared to be two members of the press, while a small nude figure approached them and began waving its arms about wildly. Unaware of these proceedings, Starlight began to address the camera:

A tax on the wealthy is a terrible mistake. It is also a bad idea. The less money a rich person has, the less he can afford to pay the poor people who do chores around the house. Poor people need the wealthy, depend on them. If it weren't for rich people, there wouldn't even be any poor people at all . . .

Behind her, the figure began chasing the frightened snackers around the yard as the camera focused in.

Poor people are used to having less and less money while rich people are used to having more and more. This tax would not only be a blow to the very fabric of our society, the rich, it would also come as a terrible shock to the poor. After all, has anyone stopped to consider whether they'd go to the right stores . . . What are you doing?

Jerry, clad only in his green Converse hightops, chased the two latent journalists toward the podium, a black bar obscuring those parts of him considered unsuitable for family viewing.

Jerry, clad only in his green Converse hightops,
chased the two latent journalists toward the art-
deco podium.

81

*Offa my land, man, and take your surveillance machines
with you . . .
Help! Help us please!
Daddy! What on earth. . . ?*

Starlight received only two phone calls following
Emmy's broadcast, the first being from Emmy herself,
by way of apology.

"Starlight? I'm terribly sorry."

"You ought to be, worm."

"I fought hard, but we just couldn't get network ap-
proval to show your father's genitals on the air."

The next call came right after dinner, from president
of the United States Ronald Reagan:

"Charlie?"

"How did you know?" asked Starlight, astonished and
thrilled.

"I'd like to thank you personally for the patriotic
things you said the other day on channel . . . Well, on
TV. I can't remember just what I saw, but I do know I
liked it."

"I . . . I love you."

The line went dead and she feared she had frightened
the man, excited him by being so forward with her emo-
tions. Still, he *had* guessed her perfume.

Starlight rose the next morning and went to find
Hashley, who was helping Jerry rebuild the gardens,
the therapy Dr. Mead had recommended following the
aging yippie's breakdown after that last party. Only
Doc Mead's advice that he begin his therapy immediately had kept her from institutionalizing him for good.
Hashley, since his return to Scarsdale, had embraced

the project with a fervor equal to Jerry's own, and the atmosphere in the yard was often one of fierce competition.

"I say, possibly some shrubbery near the entrance, but . . . oh, do I have to come right out and say it? I'll not have the statement this space could make ruined by those silly plants you've been growing in the basement."

"But they'll kill me, man."

"Now now, Mr. O'Hara, there there. We're not all 'after you' or that sort of nonsense. Part of your recovery is learning about compromise, accepting outside guidance until you're better. Look at me—I've had to accept that I haven't what it takes to make it in today's real world, but I've discovered in the process how important my art is to me. If you could only accept how important my art is to me, we could really accomplish something here. My God, man—just look at what Yoko was able to do in Central Park!"

"She didn't promise some extremely tough dudes she would deliver something Sean proceeded to set fire to—there are certain parameters here. Now I figure we can fit fifty, maybe sixty good-sized plants . . ."

"Daddy," said Starlight sternly, coming around the side of the house, "I'd like to speak with Hashley . . . alone."

"I'll be in the basement, man."

"Oh Starlight," said Hashley, visibly drained by his experience with Jerry. "What do you think becomes of people when their sense of good taste deserts them? Those who have friends in galleries or subscriptions to the right magazines come through all right. Those who don't are winnowed out. Organic themes have been out

83

for eons, you know, but there's no hope of explaining that to your father, I'm afraid."

"Oh, Hashley . . . take me!"

"Where?"

"Right here!"

"But you're already here, Starlight, don't you see?"

In another age, Starlight might have smiled demurely from behind a fan. At another time, Starlight might have blushed to the very roots of her hair. As it was, she leapt on Hashley and knocked him to the ground. He tried to pry her off with the same hoe he used to uproot the bushes Jerry planted nightly by the light of the moon.

Just as she tore his shirt open, a horn blast to the tune of "Dixie" alerted her to the rare presence of company. Running out the front door, she felt as if she were dancing on air, lost in a dream. There in the drive was a black BMW stretch touring car. It was waxed impeccably and decorated in a distinctive motif—small American flags flying over all four lights, NRA stickers lining the front and rear bumpers, the car she always knew she'd one day see, the car of Mr. Ronald Reagan himself!

"Stop that wobbling, you, and get over here."

"Yes sir, Mr. President! I didn't mean to offend you, here today or last night." There was laughter from within—woman's laughter. Oh God, the man had brought Nancy!

"We're moving in. How soon can you leave?"

"But . . . what's wrong with the White House?"

"We like these colors better."

Why wouldn't that Nancy stop giggling?

From inside the house, Jerry saw the car. He knew

what was on his property and he knew there was work to be done. He went back down to the basement, dressed himself in his finest riding leathers, and proceeded to the garage. Perhaps the sound he made when he came tearing out was no match for his old chopper's racket, but the scream he let out when the lowered garage door clotheslined him was more than enough to get the attention of everyone at Tarot. He was stunned, clearly, but he got back on his scooter and pedaled the motor back to life. The BMW spun out and headed off down the driveway with Jerry in close pursuit.

"No, Daddy—stop!" screamed Starlight. "You don't understand!"

As usual, Starlight was right. Jerry would believe for the rest of his life that he was running Richard Nixon off his land. He would never understand, as Starlight had when the back window lowered to afford a better view of the onslaught, that he was after his old butler Yamamoto and his newfound companion, Emmy Slandery. Poor child of a simpler time, rolling stone, ramblin' boy, he couldn't have been expected to know that the overalled men in the red pickup truck on the highway weren't the CIA goons of his midday dreams. But he should have had the sense to know that when a two-ton Ford flatbed pulls up beside your own much smaller vehicle, letting the bird fly is suicide. So died Jerry O'Hara: head out on the highway, bike by the side of the road.

"The sixties were great!" chirped Yamamoto into his cellular phone as Emmy undressed on the seat across from him. "The sixties were fun."

"The sixties sucked," said Brett on the other end.

So died Jerry O'Hara: head out on the highway,
bike by the side of the road.

"Oh, come now. I don't remember a single bad thing that happened in the sixties."

"Oh? But what was so great about them?"

"I can't remember that either," laughed Yamamoto. "In truth, I don't remember a single thing that happened. If I could only say the same for the eighties, I'd be a happy man."

Chapter
TWELVE

THE burden of the past lays on top of us—a heavy weight. Only constant cleaning, the physical removal of what is left behind, allows us to get on with our lives. Where would we be without the cleanings, spring, summer, fall, and winter, each special in its own special way?

The days that followed Jerry's last ride were witness to an orgy of cleaning unrivaled in Tarot's history since Jerry commissioned the Merry Pranksters to turn the nineteenth century home into the world's first tie-dye colonial two decades before. Reconstruction had begun, and Starlight was determined not to leave even a single stone unturned.

"I knows dat what de fathers build de chillums throws away," Chamois sighed, fingering the tall glass container atop the steadily mounting pile of refuse in the front yard, "but yo' daddy rather see Bill Moyers on television dan to see dis Peter Max lava lamp in de trash."

"What do you want me to do," Starlight snapped back, sending the limited collectors series John and Yoko wedding lithographs flying at Chamois's head, "dedicate a wing in the Smithsonian?" She tossed a gaily decorated plastic tube on the pile.

"Oh Miss Starlight," Chamois gasped, "Bobby Weir done take a hit from dat bong. Yo Daddy's heart be broke to pieces he see it disrespected so."

"Housecleaning," Starlight hummed, carrying yet another armload of artifacts that would doubtlessly bedevil archaeologists from some future age. "Not that you'd know anything about the subject. If only we'd done this ages ago, we wouldn't be in the fix we're in now. Kennedy buttons, Fair Housing, the Voting Rights Act . . . Out, all of it."

Chamois shook her head sadly. "I suppose I ain't surprise. Eben' de Grateful Dead play environmental benefits dese days."

"Selfish old fool," Starlight grumbled. "If he'd really cared about us, he'd have seen to it that he was fully insured."

Chamois chuckled knowingly. "Is some folks what be smart enuff fo' to take out de policy deyselves, 'specially when de person in question refuse to wear dey helmet. Course, dey is folks who 'spects others to do dey work fo' them."

"You mean to say you filled out a life insurance policy for my father with yourself as sole beneficiary?"

Chamois looked offended. "After all Massah Jerry done do fo ol' Chamois, I thought it was the leas' I could do fo' him."

"Chamois!" Starlight exclaimed. "He was my father! That money belongs to me!"

89

"Hush, chile," Chamois soothed her angry charge. "I know dat Massah Jerry don' want his precious chile spoil', dat's all."

"My father! My money!" Starlight screamed.

"Hush chile," Chamois repeated. "You hardly know he was yo' father at all, way you treat him while he was alibe. And even if you knew it, I lays ten to one odds he didn't, not most of the timbe. Now you hush, 'less you want Chamois to slap a lien 'gainst de estate."

"But where am I supposed to get the money to replace the beanbag furniture with something that matches the wallpaper?" Starlight wailed.

"I espects the Good Lawd will provide," Chamois said. "He always do in de case of yo' kine ob folks. Leas'ways dat's de way I figures it, 'cause de money sho' come from somewhere."

"That's not the Lord, that's General Dynamics," Starlight snapped. "And the only thing they have in common with God now is that neither one pays dividends."

"Why don' you asks Brett Butler fo' it den?" Chamois asked. "He always seem to hab' money."

"Brett's in prison for trading on inside information," Starlight said. "What good can he do me?"

"Whole country be run from behin' bars dese days," Chamois answered. "Mos' corporations hold dey board meetings dere, on account ob dat's de only way dey gets a quorum."

"Aren't they ashamed?" Starlight asked.

"Ashambed?" Chamois answered. "Dey don' let you hab a seat on de Exchange dese days 'less you done time. And I ain't talkin' 'bout community serbice neither—I means time in de hole. Dat's why Chamois hab to do all her banking by phone."

Struck by the force of a rare idea, Starlight rushed upstairs and returned several minutes later clad in a sheer
black Isaac Mizrahi dress. "You like?" she asked.

Chamois stared at her, disapproving. "Beggin' fo'
money in de likes o' dat be like Liz Taylor askin' fo'
food—maybe she hungry, but she sho' don't look like
she need it."

"Chamois, what do poor people wear?"

"Why, things they find round de hombre."

"Like Tupperware?"

"It make a mighty fine bonnet fo' sho'."

"I don't have a thing to wear!" Starlight wailed.

"You gots to 'conomize den. If you puts up some o'
dem stockholder certificates on de wall 'stead o' buyin'
paper from Laura Ashley, you hab money sho' 'nuff."

Starlight looked downcast as Chamois savored her tri-
umph. If worse came to worst, Chamois thought, she
could always pay the taxes out of the spare cash she kept
in her bedroom. But for now, she rather enjoyed the
spectacle of her former charge attempting to make it on
her own. The end result should finally settle one of the
Darwinian controversies closest to her heart: whether
outmoded species are capable of finding a niche in a
changed ecological landscape or will inevitably die out,
leaving only a fossil record behind. With so much at stake
it seemed wrong to interfere, so Chamois made a silent
promise to herself that after one last suggestion she'd
leave well enough alone.

"Why don' you makes use of de wallpaper den?"
Chamois slyly suggested.

"Poor people wear wallpaper?" Starlight asked in as-
tonishment.

"Sho," said Chamois, warming to her newfound

theme. "Po' peoples wears whatever dey finds at hand. Poor peoples buys off de rack at Alexanders."

Starlight weakened at this, but quickly regained her composure. "I'll do whatever is necessary to redecorate Tarot properly," she said calmly. "I'll do whatever you say."

"Alright den," Chamois said, running into the living room where the wallpaper and paste sat ready. "Now strips down so I can puts the paste on."

"Paste?" Starlight blanched.

"You been rich too long," Chamois spat. "How else you expects de paper to stick to yo' body?" she explained.

"I'm sorry," Starlight apologized. "It's just that living this way is new to me."

"Oh, I expects you gets de hang ob it soon 'nuff," Chamois soothingly replied as Starlight stripped down. "Dis' solve another problem too."

"What problem?" Starlight inquired.

"De problem you hab' wid takin' off yo' clothes."

"I never have trouble doing that," Starlight protested.

"Now you will," Chamois chuckled, "an' if you dries fast, we can make de four-fifteen to Danbury."

"You're coming with me?" Starlight asked.

"I wouldn't miss it for all de worl'."

Half an hour and three coats of paste later, Chamois turned Starlight sideways and half-propelled, half-carried her through the front door to the train station. As she lifted the stiff, prone body into the overhead baggage compartment, Chamois could hardly contain her excitement. Used to be you had to visit the White House to see so many convicted felons in a single place.

Nothing in Starlight's short lifetime of experience prepared her for the horrors that awaited at the Danbury Federal Penitentiary. *The sick beasts,* she thought, *the animals.* After all these men had been through. And the apartments! True, the brownstones were tasteful, but each one was shared by several men. And someone had put a nasty barbed-wire fence through the middle of the fairway on the sixteenth hole.

"Starlight O'Hara Hamilton and Chamois to see Mr. Brett Butler," Starlight said, announcing her party to the bespectacled clerk at the front desk. He gave her a curious glance.

"You from New York?" he asked.

"How did you know?" Starlight asked.

"No reason," he said, eyeing her costume. "Mr. Butler's in the trading room right now with the warden."

"With the warden?" Starlight asked.

"Oh, many people react that way," the bespectacled man said apologetically, "a brake on free enterprise and all. But most of our guests are used to the warden by now. It's no small matter of pride to him that some of the prisoners say he's better than the SEC."

"Where de guns?" Chamois asked.

"On the skeet range."

"I means de guns for de guards to shoots the prisoners when dey bescapes," Chamois said, perceiving the need to be somewhat more precise.

"Escape?" the desk clerk replied in true wonderment. "Why would anyone want to escape? It's only an hour to Manhattan by commuter rail."

"Dese peoples is dangerous criminals!" Chamois burst out. "And Chamois be damned if her hard-earned tax dollar be payin' for dey fancy apartments and dey Amtrak tickets."

"Oh no, Miss," the clerk hastened to reassure her. "The prisoners pay for everything themselves."

"Why dey sittin' in de trading room 'stead o' breakin' rocks in de sun?" Chamois asked, barely mollified.

"Lady, without bankers our economy would collapse!"

"Last I heard, it already did," Chamois replied.

The clerk's expression hardened. "Au contraire! All leading indicators are up for the seventh month in a row. Housing starts increased four-tenths of one percent in May. We're in a postindustrial economy now—"

"Reason it be call post-industrial," Chamois interjected, "is dat all de industry be gone." And with that Starlight and Chamois headed for the trading room.

The prison uniform was simple yet classic: Brooks Brothers 345 gray pin-striped suit, Bloomingdales white pinpoint oxford, and a rep tie. So attired, the convicts sat by consoles equipped with computer terminals and multiple phone lines and yelled across the room, placing orders and occasionally trying to sneak a peek over each other's shoulders. In short, the trading room was much like the trading rooms to be found at any of New York's major investment houses, save the usual sartorial distinctions of rank.

Starlight easily located the warden, whose potbelly and sagging jowls immediately marked him as a man who had gone for years without a corporate health club. But where was Brett? Starlight searched in vain for the elegant, commanding presence she remembered so well. In desperation, she approached the warden.

"So when this here number is ten points more than this number I press the yellow button, right?"

Brett Butler and the other convicts sat by consoles
equipped with computer terminals and multiple
phone lines yelling across the room placing
orders.

"Right," replied the hunched figure at the console. "Give it a try."

The warden pressed the button. "How much did I make this time?" he asked.

"Fifty thousand dollars," said the man at the console.

"Hot damn!" the warden bellowed.

"Excuse me, Warden," Starlight interrupted. "I wonder if you could help me. I'm looking for a friend of mine, Brett Butler. Have you seen him?"

When the man at the terminal turned around to face her, Starlight felt a tug of recognition. A snow-white beard hung down to the first button on his jacket and his face was heavily lined, especially around the eyes. She knew this man from somewhere, but where? Suddenly, a bell rang in her head.

"The prophet Jeremiah?" she quavered.

"I am Brett Butler," he answered.

Starlight shrieked and toppled over.

"Don' you eber watch de news?" Chamois said, helping her to her feet. "All de billionaires what be convicted o' securities fraud grow de long beard like Grizzly Adams. Dat's how you tell dem from de regular folks what be convicted fo' serial killings and such."

Starlight smiled uneasily at Brett and shook her head. "My word," she sputtered, "but you did give me a shock."

"Now Starlight," Brett began, annoyed, "we know each other far too well for this kind of pretense. I know that you want money from me, or you wouldn't have come here. Hell, I know you want money from me because you always want money from me and there's no reason today should be any different. The answer is no."

Turning on her heel, Starlight shuffled toward the door

with Chamois close behind. "I'll show them!" she hissed, "I'll show them all!"

"I'm sure you will, chile," Chamois replied. "But please don' do it now. Ol' Chamois seen jus' 'bout enough ob you fo' one afternoon."

Starlight pouted on the train back to Scarsdale. Her situation, quite clearly, was unbearable. Redecorating properly was beyond her means. What was she to do?

Her reverie was interrupted by an argument two rows ahead. "What do you mean, ticket?" a voice protested. "My family rides these rails free of charge!"

"Let's see some ID then, son," the conducter grudgingly requested. "Can't tell these days who is and who isn't." Satisfied, the conducter moved down the aisle.

"Used to be they let us run the country," the passenger grumbled. "Now all we get is an Amtrak pass and five dollars admission for us and our friends before eleven at Palladium."

The man in front stuck his head over the seat, and Starlight immediately recognized the lantern jaw and brown cowlick. She went warm with pleasure, for she finally saw the solution to all her problems.

"Bubba Kennedy!" she screamed, climbing down out of the rack.

"Who the hell?" he grunted, turning around in his seat. "Oh, hi Starlight."

"Let's get married!" she squealed at him, as Chamois hid in embarrassment. "What do you do?"

"I have a little store in Soho," he replied. "Greene Street. Not much, but it's a steady living. Your sister and I are going to get hitched when she gets out of Hazelden and run it together."

"It's settled then—you'll marry me instead."

"But I don't like you," Bubba protested, "I don't like you at all. I don't find you attractive in the least."

"I'll never get out of here otherwise. This marriage is purely a matter of convenience."

"Convenience?" Bubba asked.

"Yes," Starlight replied. "Mine. Marriage never, never helps my husbands."

"What ever happened to the Protestant ethic?" asked Yamamoto of his poolside cellular phone.

"You mean only associating with people from the same socioeconomic background as you?" cracked Brett.

"Yeah," Yamamoto wearily responded. "I could never be bothered to figure that one out."

Brett sighed. "I'll have my secretary look it up and call you in the morning."

Chapter
THIRTEEN

WHEN I lived in the East Village, my friends and I dreamed of nothing but art, art and nothing but. Oh, to give up our humdrum lives, and serve none but the muse who perchance may whisper in our ear at night. In the years since I've learned that even a small crafts store will do—the guiding principle remains the same.

Yes, things were looking brighter for Starlight O'Hara Kennedy. The steady cash flow from Bubba's JFK 'n' Things allowed her to shop as intensely as she always had. And marriage itself provided the security of knowing a decent divorce lawyer could get her at least half of whatever Bubba was worth. Yet, for all her plotting, she had failed to do the one thing that really mattered anymore—to get involved. If the rich are better than you or me, it is because they care. Thus it was that Starlight began spending her days at Bubba's store, completely immersed in the day-to-day struggle to turn a buck.

She learned quickly that there wasn't much to learn about her husband's business. Foreign businessmen descended upon the small shop by the busload, willing to buy anything with even the vaguest connection to Old Glory. Bubba's game was to steer them toward the most expensive items. Starlight's first real contribution was to make all the items expensive.

"I will not be seen shopping in a store that sells anything for less than fifty dollars. Why should I be seen working in one that does?"

Bubba did not want to lose the steady business they did selling tin-plated statues of liberty and such in the five-dollar range, but Starlight showed him how any large rise in prices could easily be justified by a small rise in costs. She called the Gallagher Temporary Employment Agency and set the "meats" they sent over to scraping off the Made in Taiwan stickers that adorned ninety percent of the store's merchandise.

Here was the yuppies' first opportunity in several months to do what they had been programmed to do since birth—compete ruthlessly among themselves, no matter how small the potential spoils. They leapt at the crates of JFK busts, space shuttle models, and Ronald Reagan T-shirts with a ferocity Starlight found remarkable at minimum wage. If they kept this up, no one would dare accuse her of being lazy.

By the time she returned to the front, Bubba was already entertaining the day's first customers, a junket of Japanese corporate types wearing Los Angeles Raiders caps, black Agnés B. motorcycle jackets, and thirty-five millimeter cameras.

"America!" they screamed, pointing gleefully at the knicknacks on the shelves and snapping pictures of one another in front of an autographed picture of the PT109 crew. "America!"

"Only four hundred ninety-nine dollars and ninety-nine cents," said Bubba. "Signed by Johnny K. himself, the day before Joe, Sr., had the ship sunk and bought his boy the presidency. Make me an offer—nothin's written in stone 'cept the RFK grave marker in the corner."

Starlight knew there was some truth to his words. The signature on the photo, for example, was in felt-tip—she had seen him sign several others just like it. "Take it easy," said Bubba. "There's plenty to go 'round . . ."

"*Bubba!*" yelled Starlight.

"That is to say—I got other items you fellas might find of interest." He pointed to what appeared to be a soiled rag hanging from the ceiling as every jaw in the room dropped in awe. "That there is the very jockstrap worn by Bobby the K himself during every touch football game ever played in Hyannisport."

Bubba got the jockstrap down with a pool cue he claimed had been whittled by Minnesota Fats, and auctioned all three items off as a single lot. When it was over, he accepted a check from the winner for nearly one hundred thousand dollars and handed the picture and pool cue to Starlight to wrap. The elated customer insisted on wearing his third prize out of the store.

Unable to convince any of the downtown gallery owners that his work in Tarot's garden was significant or even vaguely interesting, Hashley had been forced to consider a change in both oeuvre and locale.

"We're thinking Santa Fe," he announced one night over dinner at Lucky Strike. "I desperately need the seclusion if my acrylic work is going to improve, and the galleries there will sell anything with more than three colors in it."

"Of course," said Melody, batting her lashes shyly, "we realize it's as much your decision as ours."

"You can't go!" Starlight screamed, leaping to her feet. How could they do this? How could they take her Hashley away to a foreign land, just when things were starting to get better? The vagaries of the artistic life were beginning to set her teeth on edge.

"But Starlight," insisted Hashley, sweat beading on his forehead in the most adorable way, "I'm afraid I've already accepted a position at a gallery there, answering the phones, being overly rude to potential customers, that sort of thing. Terribly sorry. Really."

"Call them back, damn you!" she insisted. "Tell them anything—tell them you've died. Better yet, tell them your wife has!"

"But Star—"

"Don't get me wrong," she said, sitting back down. "I'm not suggesting you lie to them."

"What Hashley is trying to say," said Melody warmly, "is that we're going to need some sort of commitment from you to make it worth our while to stay . . ."

So that was her game! Hashley was her captive—that much she had already known. Now the little bitch was demanding a ransom. And what choice did she have but to pay?

"Dinner's on me," she said, seeing no way out.

"That's very gracious," Melody responded, touching Starlight's knee under the table, "but we were actually thinking of something a bit more . . . personal."

*   *   *

A week later, as Hashley directed the redecoration of the store's interior, Starlight thought back to how oddly Melody had acted on the way to that little studio on Bleecker. The cab ride could not have been fun, especially that spill onto Broadway when the door flew open at forty miles per hour. And just how many stairs did that woman have to fall down before that silly grin got wiped off her face? What was it going to take to keep that promise she had made to Hashley so long ago?

"No, people," shouted Hashley. "The stuffed eagles can't go under the Jasper Johns. Don't you see what we're about here? Think subtle, people, it's got to say subtle . . ."

The sign over the front door now read Kennedy's Boutique Americain, and unreadable auction schedules had replaced the fast-food cartons that once filled the display window. Starlight had become the consummate downtown hostess, serving each of her customers in a manner appropriate to his homeland's customs. When the windchimes over the door signaled the arrival of the day's first customer, it took her only a few seconds to guess his nationality. Impeccably dressed, absurdly thin mustache waxed lightly—definitely a Frenchman.

"Bonjour, monsieur. I've got crepes in the back, if you'd like."

"Looks to me like there's plenty in front, thank you."

"Brett!" she gasped. "How did you get out of jail?"

"Bush won. If Dukakis had, I'd be going back in a couple of weeks."

"Win some, lose some," she sighed.

"You disgust me. Look around you—what you're doing here is wrong! America is not something you can package and sell to any man with a smile on his face and a few yen in his pocket. You can't sell pieces of the U.S.A. like so much . . . like so much—"

"Corporate interest?"

"No! Absolutely not—that's something entirely different."

"Is it true what they say about homosexual rape in our prison system?"

"You're missing the point—"

"Yes, but did you?"

Brett could contain himself no longer. He flew into a rage, shredding everything that Hashley and his decorators had done to the store over the last several days. When finished, he stormed out. Starlight looked at Hashley, tears beginning to well up in his fagged, bloodshot eyes.

"Let's go, people," he said.

Brett and Yamamoto sat over brandies at the tail end of lunch at the Four Seasons.

"Warhol said that in the future, everybody will be famous for fifteen minutes," Brett opined. "I say, who needs it?"

"Yes, he told me that too," Yamamoto rejoined. "One is famous for being famous, nothing else. Look at the Kennedys."

"Silly," said Brett, craning his neck for a better view. "Silly people. Their parties are great though. Went to one last week."

Yamamoto looked nonplused, but only for a moment. "I shared a house with Jack Nicholson once in Kyoto," he offered.

"Before or after he became famous?" Brett asked.

"Before."

Brett nodded, impressed.

But as the weeks passed, Starlight began to notice a gap in her life. At first she noticed small things—an unfamiliar feeling when she returned home, a certain silence at the dinner table, one less card to punch out on the time clock at day's end. Then the gap grew larger, more noticeable: the heat was shut off and a Mr. North called incessantly about the unpaid balance on her credit card. It was then that she was able to give her loss a name: Bubba. Bubba Kennedy had completely disappeared.

It would be nice if Bubba had simply etherized in the short span of time it takes to put pen to paper. But what might work as a fictional device is rarely what happens in real life, so Starlight picked up the phone.

"Brett?" Starlight asked. "Where's Bubba? What happened to my husband?"

"The same thing that happens to all Kennedys of a certain age with no official criminal record," he replied.

"He's been arrested?" Starlight asked.

"No, he's been elected to Congress."

This was truly a predicament. Should she marry Brett Butler soon and continue her flirtation with Hashley? Or should she move to Washington and serve at Bubba's side, posing for photographs with inner-city children while keeping an eye on the path to the White House? Barring some senseless yet strangely foreseeable tragedy, the choice was simply impossible . . .

Chapter
FOURTEEN

IN these cut-rate times, we are grateful for what we can get. We want Moët, but drink Diet Coke. We want dinner with the stars, but settle for tuna in a can. Not that we aren't grateful. We go to bed the same way we wake up—a day older perhaps, a bit wiser, but grateful for all the good things that have happened.

No one is more aware of this fact than that woolly beast, the American media. Given the fact that Starlight had failed to bear Bubba a single child to salute his casket as it rolled by, coverage in general had been downright decent.

"Even though he failed to do anything with his life," the *Times* sagely pointed out, "he was nonetheless a Kennedy." For once, Starlight felt, they had hit the nail right on the head. So what if, twenty years hence, no one remembered where they were when Bubba Kennedy met his end? After all, most members of the family these days could barely remember where they were at any given time.

"Look at this!" Melody exclaimed over breakfast. "The newspaper says that Bubba may have been killed by Arabs. Arabs or the Transport Workers Union."

"Why the Transport Workers Union?" Starlight asked.

"Why the Arabs?" Hashley countered.

"Some people say it was a jealous political rival," said Melody.

"He ran unopposed," Starlight responded. "The closest Bubba ever got to political was the front row at a Ten Thousand Maniacs concert.

The truth was that being married to a Kennedy had been a chore, even a third cousin so far removed from the family's main branch that the admissions officers at Harvard College had made him write a supplemental essay before admitting him. It would have been different if her husband had been John or Robert, she reflected, but a fat, balding man who couldn't even throw a forward lateral counted for little, even with her star-struck friends.

And as inconvenient as he may have been while he was alive, Bubba was turning out to be even more of a bother dead. Hardly a day went by without a phone call or letter from someone who had absolute, incontrovertible proof that her husband had been killed by rogue CIA agents, Mikhail Gorbachev, Albanian chicken farmers, poor eating habits, or committee members from the New School for Social Research's annual fund-raising campaign. It was not the price of fame Starlight minded: it was the kind of people who collected the bills.

When the phone rang later that afternoon, Starlight leapt at it. Jackie O. may have been too proud to do Kleenex ads, but Starlight would be damned if she'd let

107

this opportunity slip away. The voice on the phone, however, had something else to propose.

"It's a tender offer, Starlight. I'm not prepared to say anything more at this time."

Starlight was caught off-guard. This was truly the last thing she had expected. "I thought you'd never ask!" she gasped.

"I'm not really asking, I'm telling," Brett Butler said. "I'll be over with my counsel to lay out the facts. And don't bother preparing a poison pill," he added, "we've already taken precautions."

Suicide was the farthest thing from Starlight's mind, but she was touched to hear Brett mention it all the same. His tenderness would certainly be welcome. *Everything is proceeding according to script,* she thought. And Brett would never do anything as tasteless as covering the bar stools on his yacht in whale testicle. She was truly excited—more so than she had been in years.

Barely one minute later Brett appeared at the apartment on Bleecker Street, accompanied by a phalanx of lawyers.

"Brett," Starlight began, "I'll be glad to marry you."

"I only do hostile takeovers," he said, a note of what might have been passion creeping into his voice, "I-I just don't know any other way."

Starlight sighed. "Alright, then—whatever makes you comfortable."

"We currently control all of your assets, including Tarot," Brett began, "and there is the small matter of the luxury tax you seem to have neglected to pay."

"Be practical," Starlight said. "It was either that or fire the interior decorator."

"Be that as it may," Brett continued, "you can either

marry me or go directly to jail. Those are the rules, my dear."

"I do."

All the men broke out cigars and shook hands with Starlight and each other.

"When do we negotiate the honeymoon?" asked Starlight, beaming.

"Got the ducats right here," Brett suavely answered, pulling two gray pieces of cardboard from his pocket.

"To Zurich?" Starlight asked, eyes wide.

"To the whole world," Brett answered, "the wonderful world of video entertainment. I expect to be away for a while on business."

Several nights later Starlight awoke in a cold sweat in the Wilkes Brothers O'Hara honeymoon suite, the VCR on pause.

"Brett," she cried, "I had the most terrible dream. I dreamed that Tarot had been purchased by a developer!"

"What kind of financing?" Brett inquired, roused from his supine position on the couch.

"He turned it into townhouses," Starlight protested. "He subdivided the lawn, he put in concrete patios with gas grills! Accountants lived there, Brett, Japanese accountants with children in Little League. I must see Tarot again, now!"

"It's progress honey," Brett sleepily responded. "Big houses are a thing of the past."

No sooner did Brett wake up the next morning than he picked up the phone and called his best friend and business partner Yamamoto, collect.

"Love," Brett hummed as the wire crackled. "Love, love, love!"

"Always with the four-letter words," said Yamamoto. "How many times have I warned you about your use of the English language in polite company?"

"Love is the best way to say you're sorry," Brett explained.

Yamamoto paused, and when he spoke again his voice was soft and low. "But it doesn't have to be that way, Brett."

"I know," he sighed. "Love can be beautiful, as long as no one else is involved."

The peace and harmony of the newly formed family unit was abruptly shattered by their first sight of their new quarters in the Trump Tower. A small room had been subdivided into four "sleeping compartments" barely big enough to kennel a large German shepherd. The sole adornment was a seven-foot-tall statue of the letter *T* carved out of granite that took up most of the space in the living room. A video installation blared prerecorded quotations from the memoirs of Donald Trump.

"It's a whole new way of life, Starlight," Brett said. "The critics call it the art of the deal."

"Dat's cause de only art be to find a buyer fo' it," Chamois said with contempt. "I heard of downward mobility befo', but not at dese prices."

Brett was generally pleased with his recent acquisitions. The apartment was secure if not comfortable, and Starlight proved to be the perfect entrée to homes that once had closed their doors to him unless he was accompanied by a search warrant. But the true object of his desire continued to elude him.

"I sho' appreciates dis' fine, fine gif'," Chamois would

say, tossing his latest offering onto the steadily mounting pile of bath soaps, perfume samples, and canvas tote bags near her bed. But her confidence, not to mention her quite sizable portfolio, continued to elude him. Somehow, someway, this impasse had to be ended.

"Chamois," he began one evening after dinner, "I want you to know that I think of you as family."

"Dat ain't much of a recommendation," Chamois said, "and I done gived you my answer already: two percent."

"Chamois, be reasonable," Brett pleaded, "I have to cover my expenses."

"Ol' Chamois didn't get where she be by coverin' no 'spenses."

"I would remind you of my position in this house."

"I wouldn't tell anyone else 'bout dat if I was you. Bein' beneath Missy Starlight hardly sumptin' to spread 'round," Chamois replied. "Fact is, you de worse massa I eber seen. Chamois ain' had anything eben resemblin' insider info in three weeks."

"How about the IBM takeover attempt?"

"Massa Brett, you a grown banker. You know as well as ol' Chamois dat you was simply tryin' to move de stock to attract an institutional investor an' den unload yo' shares. IBM be overvalued fo' years!"

Brett was stumped. Clearly it was time to try a new tack.

"Chamois, you can't fool me. I know that your manner of speech is simply an ongoing joke you've played on the O'Hara's to amuse yourself. But I'm not amused. I know you've made more money in the past ten years than anyone in this country save myself."

"Well, sho' is nice to be 'preciated ebry once in a while," Chamois said. Her expression hardened.

111

"OK, Chamois," Brett sighed. "We'll charge you a two-percent management fee for all income on your portfolio."

Chamois smiled. "Thank you, Massa Brett," she purred. "Dat surely take a load off my mind. Maybe you ain' so bad after all."

Chapter
FIFTEEN

"OH Brett, isn't it beautiful?"

Starlight bobbed in the shallow end of the indoor swimming pool at the New York Athletic Club with a dozen other pregnant women, preparing for the miracle of life's endless renewal.

"It's disgusting," answered Brett, leaning against the tiled wall in a shamefully small Old Glory–motif Speedo and a green alligator shirt, "At least on a whale watch they can't talk back to you."

"Mr. Butler," said the Underwater Lamaze instructor, a stout, hairy midwife in a faded brown one-piece from Sears, "don't you think you should be in here with the other husbands, helping your wife?"

"Helping her do what—learn how to drown a child? There'll be plenty of time for that later, in the privacy of our own bathtub."

"She needs help with her breathing, Mr. Butler."

"*Her* breathing—what about the child's? What kind of a world is it where an infant's reward for crawling its way out of the womb is a lungful of chlorine?"

"The water in the birthing tub is not chlorinated, Mr. Butler."

"Then how the hell will anybody be able to see what's going on down there?"

"The doctor will be able to *feel* how the birth is progressing, Mr. Butler. That's what's important, after all."

"That's perverted and I will not stand for it!"

"Ooohh!" shrieked Starlight, flailing around in the water. "Uhhhhhh!"

"If you're not going to contribute anything intelligent to this discussion," Brett yelled at her, "then shut up. On second thought, just shut up."

"Uhhhhh! Aaaahhh!" she screamed, churning about.

"It's time!" yelled the midwife. "Positions, everyone."

"I want to be the shark," whined Brett. "I was a minnow last time."

"No, Mr. Butler. Your wife has gone into labor."

"What are you talking about? She's never done an honest day's work in her life."

"Aaaahhhhrrrrrgh!"

"She's about to."

They lifted her out of the pool and half-carried, half-dragged her over to the whirlpool, as there was no way to get to the proper facilities in time. Unfortunately, it was occupied by a couple of nude, chardonnay-sipping lovers.

"I'm afraid we're going to need use of the whirlpool," the midwife said. "This woman is about to give birth."

"Wow," said the woman as they vacated the premises, "I've done some pretty wild stuff in hot tubs, but I've never gone *that* far."

114

*　　*　　*

After her ordeal at the NYAC, Starlight began what she hoped would be a long, slow recovery in the master bedroom of their Trump Tower condominium. She had successfully delivered a child that, once located at the bottom of the tub, proved to be a relatively healthy female.

"Isn't she just the most beautifulest wittle fing?" cooed Brett, cradling the infanta in his arms. "Just the sweetest wittle baba in the whole world."

"Look on de puny side, ef you ax me," said Chamois, turning sideways to get through the bedroom door. "Ole Chamois wouldn' be s'prise ef she wona dem crack babies you be readin' 'bout from timbe to timbe. No one to blambe dough, whet wif po' fambly structure an' all."

"Nonsense, Chamois," said Brett defensively. "Why, just look at the red in those cheeks."

"When she ole 'nuff to know jes how mech money her pa done made off de sweat ob de po' man, I 'speck it git worse."

"That's quite enough, Chamois! Don't you ever speak of such things in my daughter's presence again!"

"Whas' de harm in learnin' her 'bout de plight ob de po' man?"

"I don't want her marrying one."

"Den you betta sen' de chile to another country, 'less you plannin' on marryin' her yo'self."

"Ahem," said Starlight, sitting up in bed. "Since the two of you obviously intend to keep me from sleeping, I'd like to suggest a name."

"No!" yelled Brett, startling the child and making it cry. "See what you've done? You've scared her—she

115

wants *me* to name her, not you. She doesn't even like you."

"You have a name in mind?"

Just then, Melody walked into the bedroom carrying the *Wall Street Journal*.

"Fannie Mae!" shouted Brett, eyeing the paper, "Fannie Mae Butler!"

"That's the most ridiculous name I've ever heard in my entire life."

"Don't you dare insult my daughter," he yelled, moving toward the door. "She has a better gene pool than you."

Marriage and children bring with them surprises. Starlight was surprised to learn from Chamois that Brett was interested in having another child. Not long afterward, she was shocked to discover that he intended her to bear it.

"Isn't Fannie great?" he said cheerfully, coming into the bedroom where Starlight was still recovering from her ordeal at the NYAC.

"She's great big, is what she is. I wish you'd stop feeding her all that chocolate."

"But she likes chocolate."

"You just want her to like you."

"If I gave you chocolate would you like me?"

"No, but if you gave me a divorce maybe I wouldn't hate you so much."

"Touché. Listen, my dear—I've been thinking. Let's have another baby. What do you say?"

"Get the hell away from me."

"Another baby might be just the thing our marriage needs."

116

"The only thing our marriage needs is an anullment."

"Why, just the other day I was looking at Fannie and I realized what a miracle the creation of new life really is."

"It's a miracle you managed the first time, Brett. I can't believe you want to go through that struggle all over again."

"Don't you *dare* question my manhood!"

"I'm not questioning it, Brett, I'm just pointing out that it doesn't work very well."

"Be that as it may, another child could really improve my relationship with the IRS. I take it you understand how that in turn will improve your relationship with Saks."

"Forget it. I refuse to go through that again. There's nothing beautiful or exciting about it, Brett. Why is it that men can't understand that? It's disgusting, it's dirty, it's humiliating; it's a nauseatingly empty experience, and more than anything else, it's incredibly hard work."

"Oh come on now, Starlight—having a child's not all that bad is it?"

"I'm talking about fucking you, Brett. Once was enough."

Before long, Brett was hitting the gallery party circuit quite heavily. He donated a wing to the Met for the purpose of providing space for performance artists, whom he told the directors he wanted "off the streets once and for all." He was unanimously elected to the Board.

As for Fannie, she continued to eat everything that came within ten feet of her, and as she grew so did her demands.

"I want Barbie."

"You have Barbie."

"I mean Raggedy Ann."

"I don't want you eating granola and following the Grateful Dead around when you're eighteen."

"I want Atari."

"You have Atari."

"I mean Nintendo."

"You have Nintendo. You have Nintendo stock."

She was the first kid in the building to have whatever it was every other kid in the world couldn't have, and for the first three years of her life she prided herself on the fact. Many was the time her teacher at the Dalton School called to complain.

"Mr. Butler, I'm afraid Fannie has been teasing the other children again. She's started pointing at the school bus every time she sees it, laughing at anyone who gets on or off. Some of the children have started complaining to their parents, refusing to get on the bus in the morning because they're embarrassed."

"Good. Maybe they'll start sending their kids to school in limos like everybody else."

Soon Fannie's tastes took a twisted turn. She began to make demands no responsible parent would dream of meeting. Luckily for her, Daddy was not at all responsible and Mommy was always in bed, dreaming.

"I want MTV."

"Why not? Should I buy you a mink coat as well?"

"Hell no! Fur is murder. I want a leather jacket."

"What for?"

"Because I want a Harley Hog."

"That sounds like fun. I'll teach you to ride it myself—right up on the roof."

*　　*　　*

Thinking that three years was quite enough time to get over postpartum depression, Brett crossed the living room in two small strides and found Starlight's bedroom door locked.

"Open up, dammit," he screamed. "Open up this instant."

"Sorry," Starlight yelled from the bed. "Can't do it. Doc Mead says opening up is a process, not an action. Consider me 'in the process.'"

"What the hell is *that* supposed to mean?"

"Come back next year."

"And what then?"

"I'll tell you what it means."

Brett shrugged and clicked his heels together but nothing happened. He frowned.

"Listen, my dear—no lock is going to keep me out."

"You can huff and puff, Brett . . ."

He clicked his heels together, once, twice, three times, but still he remained standing outside his own bedroom, locked shut.

At the end of his rope, Brett backed into the hallway to gain an extra step, ran at the door, and plunged into it with everything he had. The lock did not give, nor did the wood veneer surrounding it, but nearly everything else in the apartment did. As Starlight's scream pierced the air, the entire wall between the bedroom and living room came crashing down on her.

Fortunately, the material used in its construction was of such little consequence that it did not hurt her in any way, but Brett was clearly in pain when he sprung to his feet like a tightly coiled spring, amazed to find himself in

119

his own bedroom for the first time in three long years.

"Good," he said, surveying the damage. "That's exactly what I'd planned to do."

"Sex," Brett proclaimed, moodily bouncing up and down on the display model waterbed Yamamoto had chosen for his inspection. "Sex is really overrated."

"Compared to what?" Yamamoto inquired.

"Oh, I don't know. A walk in the woods, a strong cup of coffee," Brett answered, turning to his sometime companion. "A good conversation with an old friend."

"Wife's not putting out," Yamamoto answered with finality. "Just relax. Forty years from now it won't matter either way."

"Sex," Brett proclaimed, moodily bouncing up and down on the display model waterbed Yamamoto had chosen for his inspection. "Sex is really overrated."

Chapter
SIXTEEN

WITH a single motion she divested herself of the things we wear: clothes. Off came her coats, hats, sweaters, pants, and dresses. On her knees she came to him—warm, soft flesh, arms, legs, eyes, all mixed up together. A gentle fumbling, muttered words, the touch of a lip, then four lips. Only two to go she thought, gently stroking him.

"Oh Hashley, it's been so long, so hard . . ."

"Sorry," he said, "I'm so very sorry, Starlight."

At that moment Emmy Slandery burst in. "Omigod, omigod, omigod!" she screamed. "Omigod—I'm telling and you two are going to be in a lot of trouble."

"Why?" Hashley asked. "Because we're married to other people?"

"No. Because you're having bad sex. People don't have bad sex in books anymore—they only have *good* sex. They have to, because no one in the real world does, no matter what they tell their friends. You two are in *big* trouble."

"You've betrayed me," Brett screamed at Starlight when she got home. "Everyone in town knows what you did this afternoon. You are unfit to be the mother of my children."

"Don't be ridiculous," laughed Starlight. "If I didn't have affairs, no one would know we're married."

The dinner party at Aunt Pat's that evening was a lively affair, and the name on everyone's lips was Starlight.

"Starlight, is it true?"

"Starlight, was it good?"

"Starlight, you have such courage. I could never have sex."

Melody was nearly as popular as she fielded a stream of embarrassingly personal questions about the exact terms of her prenuptial agreement with respect to extra-marital affairs.

"You must feel terribly inadequate, my dear," one matron offered. "Whenever my George tried something like that I'd jump on top of him every chance I got for weeks. The very thought of sex makes him ill now."

"Men," someone sighed.

"Whoa!" Doc Mead cut in, waving his arms violently in the air. "There seems to be quite a bit of hostility in the air tonight. Hold onto those feelings, and let's try to channel them into something constructive."

"Like all-out war between the sexes?" someone asked.

"Yes!" Doc Mead replied. "Everyone pair off into discussion groups. There will be absolutely no charge for the evening, and once Mrs. Mead puts on her coat and leaves, we may begin."

Groups were formed and Doc Mead shuttled from one to another, offering encouragement and advice where needed.

"Who's your ideal man?" he asked one group.

"Well," one woman responded, "I'd have to say G. Gordon Liddy."

"Why?"

"He does what he's told and keeps his mouth shut."

"And your ideal woman?" he asked a male group member.

"Cheryl Tiegs."

"Why?"

"Good point," the man allowed.

Others discussed their personal lives.

"My husband thinks of me the way he thinks of his exercise bike."

"How so?"

"He gets on for five minutes, gets red in the face, gets off, lights up a cigarette, and turns on the TV."

The women soon found, however, that they were not alone in their complaints.

"My wife is like Marilyn Monroe," one man whined.

"Really?"

"Yeah. They both died in bed in 1963."

"How about commitment?" Doc Mead asked.

"I tried that," one man answered.

"And?"

"It helped for a while, but then her parents got a second opinion and the hospital had to let her go."

Doc Mead finally called a halt to the discussion. "I have the solution to the problem at hand," he announced, turning to the two troubled couples. "Starlight and Melody must sleep together."

"What the hell are you talking about?" Brett asked.

"Jealousy," Doc Mead explained. "The problem here is misaligned jealousies. Melody is jealous of Starlight for sleeping with her husband. Starlight is jealous of Melody for being Hashley's wife. Brett is jealous of Hashley because Starlight obviously prefers Hashley. Hashley is jealous of Brett because . . . well . . . because . . ."

"What the hell is your point?" Brett asked.

"If your wives sleep with each other," Doc Mead continued, mopping his brow, "you'll be jealous of them for making it with a woman while you didn't get to watch. That way, each of you will be jealous of your wives and scared that they are secretly lesbians, which is as close to a definition of normalcy in marriage as I'll ever get."

"I think Doc Mead has a point," Melody meekly offered.

"I agree," said Brett, "and if you ask me he reached it several Scotches ago."

The normally quite pacific atmosphere at the Elephant and Castle was disrupted by a loud and discordant trumpeting noise.

"Goddammit!" Brett Butler yelled, pounding his fist on the table, sending his fresh-squeezed orange juice leaping to the very brim of his glass.

"Your order will be ready in a minute sir," a white-clad waiter replied without missing a beat.

Brett sighed. "Look at them," he said, the sweep of his arm encompassing a clear majority of the diners present. "Receding chins, fat cheeks, faces like merengue pie."

"Ah," Yamamoto reflected. "The sins of the fathers are visited upon the sons."

125

"And so is their money," the waiter interjected, refilling their cups with hot, black coffee.

When Starlight failed to return home that evening, Brett scooped up Fannie Mae and purchased two full-fare tickets to London. Fannie Mae had grown into a remarkable young child who had aged several years in the space of only ten short pages, and was no longer eligible for the half-price youth fare.

"Daddy, why are we going to London?" she asked as the Concorde carried them across the Atlantic.

"Remember Big Ben from your storybooks?"

"I hate storybooks. Is Boy George in London?"

"I don't know."

"Is London where Ric Astley and the Pet Shop Boys live?"

"Who's to say?" Brett replied.

"Then why are we going to London?" she asked.

"Because Mommy is a pervert," Brett explained. "Now shut up and eat your trail mix."

"If she's afraid you'll tell, she should just kill a pony and make you watch," Fannie Mae logically explained. "That's what the teachers do at school."

"Don't tell lies, Fannie," Brett soothed. "You know those teachers were acquitted."

After a few days in London, Fannie Mae began to tire and complain.

"Daddy," she said one night. "I have bad dreams at night. I dream that a man with a mustache touched me in my secret place when I was asleep."

"What did he look like?"

"Oh Daddy, he looked exactly like you." Fannie Mae burst into tears.

Brett looked long and hard at his daughter. "I think you're lying," he said slowly. "I don't think my little girl had those dreams at all."

"Maybe they weren't dreams then," Fannie Mae suggested. She had suddenly stopped crying.

"Fannie, you know what happens to people who tell lies," Brett warned.

"Yes, Daddy," Fannie Mae smiled happily. "Their lawyers get them off."

Brett sighed. "You made up those dreams, didn't you?"

"Daddy is very smart," Fannie Mae said. "Daddy is much smarter than Mommy is."

Brett was beginning to see the light. "You mean that although Daddy knows you are lying, Mommy might not?"

"Mommy is so stupid sometimes!" Fannie Mae squealed joyously. "Daddy would never believe such silly stories if I told them to him."

"This is blackmail!" Brett yelled.

"Does that mean I get the corner office?" Fannie yelled, jumping up and down on the bed.

"That's greenmail, honey. It's very different."

"How so?" Fannie Mae asked, curious.

"OK," he said, throwing up his hands in defeat. "What do you want?"

"I want us to go home, now. Cable here sucks, and the doorman told me that Johnny Depp and Winona were going to be on MTV."

Brett and Fannie Mae celebrated their return to New York the same way they celebrated all special occasions, stopping by Rumplemeyers for hot fudge sundaes. As al-

127

ways, Brett snuck out the front door while Fannie Mae pretended to cry. This simple trick never failed to amuse the girl, Brett reflected with pride. And why not? Lee Iacocca used the same technique with Congress during the Chrysler bailout, and now he's a multimillionaire.

That afternoon in the lobby of Trump Tower, Fannie Mae suddenly stopped and pointed. "Look Daddy," she yelled. "It's Mommy!"

Starlight purpled with anger when she saw them. "How dare you take my child away from me," she screamed, flailing at him wildly with her Gucci handbag. "You don't care what becomes her!"

"I just spent an entire week with her in London," Brett said.

"London!" Starlight gasped. "Next thing you know you'll be taking her to clubs."

"What's wrong with England?" Brett asked.

"The food is awful" Starlight said, shaking her fists. "You'll ruin her palate!" Starlight screamed, missing Brett with a tremendous swing of her handbag and toppling headlong down the escalator.

"Now you've done it," she sobbed when Brett reached her. "You've torn my Scaasi. There'll be no second child, no matter how the tax code changes this year."

Fannie Mae burst into tears. "A second child? Does it get part of my trust fund?"

Starlight and Brett stood on the sidewalk in front of Trump Tower overseeing Fannie's Sunday afternoon riding practice.

"Goddammit, Fannie," screamed Brett, "not all at once—it's not like in the movies. Don't give her any more than she absolutely needs. You've got to concentrate to stay on."

"Brett," sulked Starlight, "you're acting just like one of those high-pressure parents Doc Mead is always complaining about."

"Good for Fannie! Good for Fannie!" yelled Brett, as his daughter fell to the pavement.

A loud roar from somewhere up Fifth Avenue became audible.

"Let's get the hell out of here," Brett nervously suggested. "Those are tanks, dammit. Tanks are rolling down Fifth Avenue."

"What about Fannie?"

"She'd only slow us down."

Before the matter could be resolved, however, a sea of Hell's Angels came rumbling into view. Starlight looked frightened. "It's Malcolm Forbes's funeral procession," she said. "Now everyone's going to know we didn't go."

Fannie, free from Brett's meddling, had completely mastered the beast beneath her. As the procession roared by her petrified parents, she let the clutch out on her Harley Hog and joined the fleet. Something about the peaceful look on Fannie's face told her parents she was road ready. Something about the upturned middle digit she sent their way told them they would never see her again.

"Just like Daddy," sighed Starlight.

"I like to think so."

"I'm talking about my Daddy."

"You're saying our child is like Jerry?"

"No—he is." She pointed to where, at the end of the motorcade, a ghastly hippie resembling her father was lying back on his chopper, bearing a sign that read:

You're Not Responsible, Man. They Are.

"I don't see a thing," Brett grunted.

Chapter
SEVENTEEN

WHAT you are about to read will shock you. More than that, it will surprise and sadden you. If I was not convinced it was important, I'd never have written this book. In the war between truth and discretion, truth must always be the victor.

"When is my mother going away?" asked Johnny as Hashley carried him back from yet another trip to Melody's room.

"Perhaps not for a long, long while," his father answered softly. "These devices could keep her going well into your teens."

"Why is she going away?"

"Johnny, I'm afraid your mother is no longer needed."

"Hashley," said Emmy cheerfully, looking up from her magazine, "interesting article here concerning death counseling. Have you given it any thought?"

"Well, you know Melody. When the time comes, I'm sure she'll manage."

"No, Hashley—someone to help her prepare, make peace with herself."

"Oh. Doc Mead is with her right now, but he's terribly drunk and won't let her get a word in edgewise."

"What?" barked Brett, looking at his watch. "You mean she can still talk?"

A groan went up from nearly everyone in the waiting room.

"My God," snapped Pat, "we'll never get out of here."

Doc Mead came stumbling down the hall toward them, smiling and waving his hand in the air.

"It's OK," he mumbled, hiccuping. "Everything's fine. She understands."

"Understands what?" asked Hashley.

"Everything—how devastated everyone is over this whole thing, how she's really letting you and Johnny down, what a terrible human being she's been all along."

"She said all that?"

"Of course not. But I explained it all to her and she understands now."

"I'd better go talk to her," said Emmy, getting up.

"Be reasonable, Emmy. She never liked you for beans. She wants to talk to Starlight," said Doc Mead, patting his jacket pockets and turning to Starlight, "If you see a flask in there . . ."

Melody lay perfectly still as Starlight knelt by the side of her bed. There were tubes in her arms and nose, and monitors of various functions beeped irregularly all around the room. Her face was a pale, waxy yellow and there were purple circles around her eyes. Even at death's door she looked no worse than the average girl from Long Island on a Friday night in the City.

"*Boo!*" Starlight yelled, causing the monitors to go haywire. Melody's eyelids began to twitch uncontrollably, and for a moment Starlight thought the wait was over.

"Promise me," said Melody, opening her eyes and scaring the hell out of her guest.

"What? Promise you what?"

"Promise me you'll never do that again."

"OK, OK. I promise."

"And look after my little son."

"Sure. Whatever."

"College?"

"Don't worry—I'm sure he'll qualify for financial aid."

"And Europe?"

"Maybe he could take a semester abroad—he'll have to arrange that himself, though."

"And a pet of some sort?"

"For God sakes, Melody, I can't do *everything* for the boy!"

"And promise me you'll be kind to Brett—he loves you so."

"Brett Butler can kiss my ass. What about Hashley?"

"He likes you so-so. Starlight, you will keep your promises to me won't you?"

"I always keep my promises," she hissed, yanking the pillow out from under Melody's head and covering her face.

"Mmmmmph!"

"What now?" asked Starlight, removing the pillow momentarily.

"Tell Hashley the insurance forms are in the top drawer of the rolltop desk."

"Fine," she snapped, applying the pillow again.

"Death," Brett flatly exclaimed. "What a meaningless waste of life."

Yamamoto clucked sympathetically. "A sad fate," he agreed, "but consider the alternatives."

"I just don't see the purpose of it," Brett whined.

"Meaning is relative," Yamamoto explained. "Life would be meaningless without death."

"Yeah, but it sure would last longer," Brett replied, hanging up the phone and returning to the waiting room in time for the official announcement from Doc Mead.

"Dead enough for me."

A muffled cheer went up among the waiting room crowd, and all but Hashley and Starlight rushed down the hall and into Melody's room to satisfy their morbid curiosity.

"Can I touch her?" asked little Johnny.

"Sure," said Brett. "We all can."

"Hashley! Oh my Hashley!" she gushed, throwing herself at him, "It's over—done! We can be together now."

He was weeping heavily, but still managed to sidestep her advance, causing her to fall flat on her face.

"But Hashley," she said, lifting herself off the floor, "you don't understand."

"No, Starlight," he wept, "it's you who doesn't understand. I'm not at all the man you think I am—the man you fell in love with. Don't you see? I'm not like these people—your people. I know you'll never be able to forgive me for this, Starlight, but I voted for Walter Mondale."

Brett walked by on his way out, a smug grin stretching that silly mustache across his face. He'd never looked so good, but perhaps there was still some small hope left for her and Hashley.

"Who did you vote for in eighty-eight?" she asked as he fell to his knees, sobbing uncontrollably.

"I . . . I didn't even register."

As her limousine sped down Fifth Avenue toward Trump Tower, Starlight stared out the window and thought about how foolish she'd been all these years, chasing after that no-good Hashley when all along it was Brett she loved. Brett, who sat on the boards of half the Fortune 500 corporations. Let's see, that made . . . oh, what difference did it make? Brett, with his millions safely tucked away outside the U.S. Brett, who spoke fluent Japanese and was quickly picking up German. Brett, who could give her the life she had always dreamed of, if only he would die and leave her everything.

When she reached Trump Tower, she rushed past the doorman and took the elevator up to the apartment, praying she wasn't too late.

"So," said Brett, coming out of the bedroom carrying twin Gucci suitcases, "she's dead. That must please you."

"I thought it would," she said, turning to face him, "but I don't anymore."

"Why not?"

"Because the real pleasure was in watching her die. I never really understood that until she was gone."

"She was a good woman. What did she say to you in there?"

"She said 'Brett is a bad man.'"

"Did she say anything else?"

"She said you were a terrible lay. We had a good laugh about that."

"No doubt. Well, I suppose this is good-bye. I'll have my lawyer get in touch with you."

"But Brett—you're wrong! Terribly wrong! I don't want a divorce."

"Don't worry—I'm worth far too much to divorce you, Starlight. I just figured you'd need a good lawyer once they start looking into Melody's death."

"Brett, you . . . you can't actually think that I—"

"Oh, don't worry. I won't say anything—the damage to my reputation would cost me millions."

"Oh Brett, I realize now that I must have loved you for years only I was too financially secure to realize it."

"Starlight, please don't go on like this. Leave us some dignity to remember out of our marriage." He walked out into the hallway and called the elevator as she ran after him.

"Brett!" she cried, "Brett! You've just utterly destroyed my life, my plans for us . . . What are you going to do now?"

"I'm going to Disneyland."

"Please—*please*—take me with you!"

"No way. I'm through with everything here. I want to see if there isn't something left in life of charm and grace, honor among thieves, laissez-faire capitalism—"

"What the hell are you talking about?"

"Tokyo. They're doing amazing stuff there."

"But Brett, what shall I do?"

"Frankly, my dear," he said as the elevator finally arrived and he stepped inside.

"I wish you'd quit saying that all the time—*frankly* this, *frankly* that. It's enough to give a person the impression you've never been frank about one single thing in your entire life. Why, if I had a dime for every time you've said *frankly* something . . ."

Starlight crawled around the apartment on her hands and knees for nearly an hour until she located her Ray• Bans, and once they were on she somehow gathered the strength to open her eyes.

Oh my God! she thought. *Where the hell am I? How did I get here? Oh yes, now I remember. There was a man, a mustache I was just sure was a fake. I don't want to think about him—he makes my head hurt. But there was another man as well, less money than the other but—can't think about him either, just makes me nauseous.*

She called for a limo and settled into the plush seat for the long ride to Scarsdale. Strange messages were hand painted over the road signs along the way:

Turn back!
They want you to go home, man.
Say no to their thing.

A long, low chopper was parked on the shoulder beneath each new installment, its familiar nude rider trying desperately to flag the limousine down with a badly stained pair of orange bellbottoms.

I'm going to Tarot, Starlight thought, unaware of the apparition. *Home . . . I'll go home. And I'll think of some way to get back at Brett, at all of them.*

The sun was setting, and as the silhouetted form of her once-proud home came into view Starlight realized that

Sioux-Ellen had made changes in her absence. Bullet-riddled boards covered every window, where once beautiful paisley tapestries had fluttered in the breeze. Broken beer bottles and small glass vials were strewn about the yard along with several teenagers, none of whom seemed to be moving or breathing.

"Driver," Starlight managed to say, softly but with authority, "get me the hell out of here."

Chapter
EIGHTEEN

A considerable silence ensued.

"The ending was very sad."

"The parts about black people were inappropriate, but the inversion of traditional roles while retaining the Old Southern dialect was entertaining."

"I liked Jerry. I liked how he was on drugs all the time."

"The fools, the careless fools."

Yamamoto rapped his long, metal pointer against the conference table and called for silence. "You have been privileged to witness the debut of an entirely new form of entertainment," he announced. "The success of the project is entirely my own, but I do owe Mr. Butler some thanks for providing the money—unknowingly, of course."

"None of the people knew they were being recorded?" Mr. Roki asked.

"I merely provided a scenario," Yamamoto explained. "A nudge here, a nudge there, a crazy woman who writes romance novels to fill in the blanks."

"But the people weren't told what to do?"

"Nothing was scripted, if that's what you mean. The characters' actions came from inside. Method Acting at its truest, if you will. It all goes to show that, given half a chance, Americans will gladly behave like characters in a bad romance."

"Aren't you being a bit harsh," the student with wire-rimmed glasses in the front row objected. "Human existence may be infinitely varied, but when you boil it down to its essentials, the number of plots is quite small indeed."

Mr. Roki nodded in agreement. "That point is well taken."

Encouraged, the student pressed on. "I also question the morality of such a project." Heads turned. "I mean," he stammered, "it is one thing to laugh at the misfortunes of imaginary others. It is much worse when those misfortunes are real, especially when you are somehow the cause."

A low murmur filled the room and Yamamoto rapped for silence once again. "All artistic creation is rooted in misfortune," he declared, "whether it is the misfortune of the artist, the misfortunes of people the artist observes, or the misfortune of those who pay for his work only to find they can't get their money back."

"I enjoyed this entertainment," Mrs. Roki declared. "I'll buy anything connected with *Gone with the Wind,* no matter how remote the connection. Trivia books, china plates, paper cut-out dolls, you name it. What I am most curious about is how the narrator knew what was going on inside the characters' heads."

"People talk," Yamamoto said. "People talk entirely too much."

"Even the dreams?" she asked.

"People tell their most private dreams to complete strangers," Yamamoto said. "People will stop you on the street and tell you their dreams. If you leave in the middle they'll still be standing there, talking. Freedom of information is one of the most sacred principles of American life. As is the right to make fun of turgid, overblown romances, and publisher's insistence to capitalize on a gullible nation's predilection for meaningless nostalgia."

The intercom by Mr. Roki's right hand buzzed. He leaned over and spoke a few quick, short words. "Gentlemen," he said, "I believe this dispute will be settled momentarily."

The sound of clicking heels was followed by the abrupt appearance of Brett Butler, who entered to a round of quiet giggles. He looked nonplussed.

"Why Yamamoto," Brett stammered, "so nice to see you. I had no idea you'd be here."

The tension was clearly broken and everyone in the room laughed, Mr. Roki hardest of all. "Brett Butler," he said, "why don't you explain your idea to my friends."

Brett leaned forward and straightened his tie. "If something worked once, it will work again," he began. "This is true of automobiles and movies. It is even true of Michael Cimino and Cheryl Ladd. I believe it was Joseph Goebbels who put it best: A lie told once is a lie; a lie told one million times is the truth."

"And so?" Mr. Roki prodded.

"And so," Brett continued, "I have a business proposition that may interest you and your friends. It is an idea

140

so obvious that it is a wonder no one has thought of it before. It is an idea so shallow that it will unquestionably sell big. What I have in mind is a sequel," Brett paused dramatically, "a sequel to *Gone with the Wind*."

The corners of Mr. Roki's mouth began to twitch, but he managed to suppress a smile. "But what's the point, Mr. Butler?" he asked.

"Point?" Brett asked, puzzled.

"Yes," Mr. Roki said. "Why would anyone want to write a sequel to a book that was behind the times the day it was published? Why do what's already been done before?"

"It's not a matter of anyone wanting to write the book," Brett answered. "The book is written already. It's a thing called democracy. Democracy means that whatever the people want the people get, and what the people want is someone to tell them what happened to Rhett and Scarlett after the book ended."

"But isn't that the point, that we don't know what happened?" Mr. Roki asked. "Does Raskolnikov kill again? Did Nick Carraway prefer the Whopper or the McDLT? Does Holden Caulfield become a management trainee at Goldman, Sachs and join the Elks? Mr. Butler," Mr. Roki said with some severity, "if you want to mount a frontal attack on what little ambiguity remains in the arts, you might have picked a better place to start."

"The questions you raise interest me very much," Brett said. "In fact, we have teams of writers working out the answers to them at this very moment, on spec of course. But what about *Gone with the Wind*?"

"But why?" Mr. Roki asked again. "What proof do you have that anyone is even remotely interested in reading a sequel to *Gone with the Wind*?"

"Because people are interested in anything that will take their minds off of their day-to-day lives, which, day-to-day, are quite miserable indeed. A world in which men are men, women are in the kitchen, and blacks and other troublesome minorities are firmly in their place is a world in which most Americans would rather live, if only for a few hours, than the one they wake up to every morning."

"And if you're wrong?"

"Then we'll mount a four-and-a-half-million-dollar advertising campaign and shove it down their throats," Brett replied. "It will be on the cover of every magazine in the country."

"What do you think?" Mr. Roki asked, turning to face the audience. "Should we do as Mr. Butler suggests?"

Silence filled the room. "Well," Mr. Roki said, "we all seem to be in agreement. Mr. Butler, your idea is not accepted by the group. People want something different, something they haven't seen before. Something like what we're doing now."

"Oh," said Brett. "What's that?"